Towei

MW00903121

# The Prisoner and the Traitor

Tower of the Deep Volume 1
**The Prisoner and the Traitor**

Copyright © 2021 by H. M. Richardson

Cover design by Kristen Hubschmid
Copyright © 2021
www.khubswindow.com

Edited by Katie Erickson
www.katieericksonediting.com

Published by: A Voice Crying Publishers
richheidi@gmail.com
Amazon Author Page: https://www.amazon.com/author/a.voice.crying.2022
Olds, Alberta, Canada

ISBN: 978-1-7778374-0-2

*Soli Deo Gloria*

# Chapter One

A strange ungainly bird rose high into a sky full of broken sun-splashed clouds, reached the top of an arc, and plummeted down. It was an odd bird, squashy and rounded with no wings to speak of, and very sparsely feathered. It was, in fact, not a bird - nor even a living thing at all. It was only a leather bag stuffed lightly, with a few goose feathers sewn on.

Just as it began to fall, a fine, long arrow thunked squarely into it, causing a drastic detour in its descent.

Below, four pairs of eyes watched it dive, and young voices raised a cheer for the excellent shot. Three people stood all together in a small group: a grown man, and two youngsters, a boy and girl, all dressed in brown and tan training garb and high boots. Sitting on a tree branch over them was another young male.

The man clapped the lad next to him on the shoulder.

"Very good, Wendaniko, very good! You've improved since we did those lessons on your aim."

"Thank you, sir," the boy replied, a blush rising to his pale cheeks. He was slim and slight, and his white-blonde hair rose from a center part like a fountain, fine and smooth, falling to about chin-length. He was fourteen years old.

Even the girl was sturdier than Wendaniko, yet slender and clean-limbed, like a young colt. Her long hair, almost the color of honey, was too wavy and abundant to lie in its proper place, so she had caught it up in a low ponytail for her archery exercises. She was also fourteen. The man had coarse hair, almost black, that would not lie neatly even when he was indoors, which was seldom. His olive skin was chafed red by sun and wind, his square frame packed with muscle. He squatted and placed another leather bag in the small catapult, winding up the mechanism once more.

"All right, now let us see how you do, young mistress Hennelyn," he challenged the girl with a grin. She hardly had time to lift her bow as he released the catch; the target soared into the air. Hennelyn yanked the string taut and released it quickly, making it sing. The arrow sliced after the ball, but nothing happened. The target just wilted in the air and dropped.

"Ha! A miss!" shouted the youngster in the tree with glee. "The great General Kanow's daughter scores a 'no hit'! Even Nik the gardener's son did better."

"Oh, go soak your tail-feathers," mumbled Wendaniko, known as Nik to everyone. He frowned at the implied insult.

"Come on, Ghundrew! I wasn't ready!" Hennelyn complained to her trainer.

"Ready? Mistress, in battle or while hunting, there is rarely an occasion when the quarry will stand still and wait while you take aim."

Hennelyn frowned up at the boy in the tree who was still chuckling. One side of her mouth curled up slyly.

"Ghundrew, send one up for Arcmas. I want to see how he does at a moving target," she suggested. The youngster above looked down at her and cocked his head to one side.

"For me?!" he asked. Hennelyn crossed her arms and eyed him expectantly. His grin broadened.

"Child's play."

Ghundrew started to wind the catapult again, reaching out for another target to put into it.

"Good. Come and start from here beside me, then, right from the ground," she commanded. Arcmas's smile wavered a bit, then he shrugged.

He had been squatting on the branch with his hands holding on either side of him, and in that position had looked human. But now, from behind his back, there billowed out two huge wings, and he sprang lightly from the branch and parachuted down to land on the grass not far from the others. There, away from the concealing green shade, his differences were obvious.

His face and body were shaped like any human boy of fourteen. But instead of hair, feathers adorned his head. In fact, feathers were everywhere, covering arms, chest, shins - presumably under the clothing that he wore - everywhere but his face and the front of his neck. His hands were of human shape, but the skin on them was tough and leathery, and long, sharp claws grew in place of nails. His bare feet showed not five small toes, but three long, leathery ones forward and one pointed back, armed with wicked curving talons.

His feathers were mottled nut-brown and tan, with cream on the breast and undersides. A full complement of tail feathers stuck out from under the back of the tunic he wore. Such was Arcmas, and he was the only one of his kind that he knew of.

He crouched forward, and his wings stretched to an amazing width - more than twice as wide as he was tall. The longest flight feathers vibrated slightly at their tips. Strangely, no one offered him a bow and arrow.

"I'm ready, Ghundrew," he said through clenched teeth. Ghundrew released the lever again.

Arcmas exploded into the air. The others raised arms against the small windstorm that his departure created. He almost reached the target, but it fell away from his grasp. Arcmas merely folded up his wings, and dove after it. Faster and faster he streaked down until it looked like he would dash himself into the ground. Hennelyn had seen him do this before, yet it always made her shiver.

Arcmas plunged to the bare prairie until the humped vagaries of the ground hid him from view. As the others craned their necks wondering, they saw him pop up in the distance with the bag clutched in his raised left hand and a big grin on his face. Rising into the air once again, he soared back to them and dropped lightly down next to Hennelyn. He proffered the target to her.

"I got it - in the air," he boasted smugly. Hennelyn stuck her nose up.

"This time," she allowed archly and turned her back on him. He laughed.

Hennelyn went to pick up her quiver from the grass, and Arcmas returned the target to Ghundrew. The soldier did not offer him any congratulations nor clap him on the shoulder. His glance at this strange youth was, as usual, sidelong and uneasy.

As the children gathered up their practice weapons, there was a sudden distant racket of metal clanging on metal.

"Supper! Come on, Henna, I'll race you to the castle!" cried Nik, and they set off at a run, their quivers and bows dangling from their arms. After a moment, Arcmas stepped lightly into the air and flew sedately after them.

The dwelling they approached was not really a castle, but a large two-story house, built mostly of logs and rough lumber. It looked cobbled together in a hurry, which was the truth, but sturdy and strong nonetheless. It perched on the highest, most strategic point of a long ridge on the north side of a river valley. Below it, a swift river looped

5

back and forth like a seeking snake, flowing mainly east. Just where the house was situated, the river bent closer to the ridge than it did at any other point. A small, rough town sprawled along the lower slopes between the castle and the water.

Behind the house to the north, east, and west stretched an unending bald prairie riddled with gullies and hollows where trees grew and creeks sprang out of the ground to eventually join the river, through copses of trees fully fleshed out in late summer green. A sea of grass clothed the hills, faded to brown since August, but still appetizing to horses and cattle. To the west and south across the valley, rolling hills climbed higher until they eventually formed the toes of a huge mountain range dominating the western horizon.

A wide four acres of horse-cropped grass surrounded the house, bounded by a sturdy wall of spruce logs standing upright and pointed on top, twenty feet high. At each of the four corners of the wall stood a tall lookout tower which gave the soldiers an uninterrupted view of the surrounding plains, connected by wooden walkways high off the ground; these towers were the only features laboriously built of stone. The wall enclosed all the outbuildings of the house: the servant's quarters and hall, the stables, the kitchens, the bunkhouse for soldiers when they were on duty there, and the outhouse. There was only one gate in and out, facing west to the town.

Hennelyn and Nik puffed up to the door of the house, breathless from climbing the steep hill. Arcmas drifted down beside them. This was where the three of them always parted for meals. Hennelyn and Arcmas ate with their father in the great hall; Nik would join his family in the servant's hall, where the small complement of kitchen and cleaning staff ate, along with the stable boys. But first they served the men in their bunkhouse - the soldiers presently acting as guards in the compound.

"Nik, you are not angry with me, are you?" Arcmas asked him. "That really was very fine shooting today." The shorter boy looked up at him.

"Thanks! No, I'm not angry. You did good, too. Well, goodbye, Henna, Arcmas."

"Goodbye, Nik," Hennelyn answered. "If we're out tonight, we'll give you the signal."

"Okay!" he called over his shoulder as he ran off towards the outbuildings. The other two entered the great hall through the main door on the ground floor, placed right in the middle of the longest wall. Inside, the large open room was dominated by a huge fireplace in the center and decorated here and there with the general's hunting trophies: some mounted heads and a couple of entire stuffed animals (a badger and an owl), plus a few hanging skins.

The hall was big enough to accommodate two hundred people, and sometimes it did. But right now, only General Kanow, along with the children's governess and tutor, sat at the fairly small table closest to the great stone fireplace. Despite the warm season, a cheery fire radiated the chilly hall. The sun was already tracking west, thrusting dusty, golden fingers into the room from two big unshuttered windows on that side. These windows framed the buttery evening light bathing the grounds outside. They also let in a cool draft from the waning day.

"Hello, Father!" Hennelyn cried, skipping over to him.

"Hello, sir," was Arcmas's greeting.

"Hello, children," Tai answered, smiling. He stood to give a one-armed hug to each. The other two people there showed their respect by standing up to greet the children.

Tai was a tall, strong man, even among the Starkhons who were known for their mighty warriors. His hair was dark like most of his race, and he sported an ebony mustache and goatee. The children turned next to their tutor and governess, the two of them obviously of the fair Luinian race from the south. These two were among others who had followed the Kanow family from their southern home to this wilderness.

"Good evening, Lisha," Hennelyn greeted the woman, giving her a peck on the cheek. To the tutor she nodded, "Good evening, Jaero Lite." Arcmas did the same and received his 'good evenings' as well.

Lisha's hair, as pale as Nik's, was swept up on top of her head, courtesy of the maid's clever fingers. Though small and delicate, she was constructed of angles rather than curves, her face calm and molded like alabaster. Only the tiniest of crows-feet had begun to show at the corners of her eyes, though she professed to be older than Tai Kanow.

The tutor, Jaero Lite, stood taller but still had a slight body. He reached approximately to the general's chin in height. His blonde hair had begun to fade to silver, especially about his ears. He was always clean-shaven, in contrast to his master.

They all took their places, the general with his back to the fire at the head of the table, the youngsters at either hand; the two females on one side, the two males on the other. They seated themselves all together, cueing the servants to serve the dinner. It was nothing fancy; the family ate simply most of the time. Tonight it was bread and a venison stew with gravy.

After the meal, as Hennelyn looked around expectantly for the servers, Tai Kanow broke the bad news that there would be no dessert course that night.

"Because the bunjis have disrupted the caravan that was bringing us more sugar, among other things. Most of the supplies were stolen," he told them. Hennelyn sighed with disappointment, missing her sweets.

"If only the bunjis were not so good at hiding," she complained. As the people who were already living in the area when the Starkhons arrived, the bunjis had the home advantage when it came to stealth.

"Or that they would leave our caravans alone," muttered Arcmas. But he knew enough to leave the topic alone. After two years of trouble with the mysterious locals, no one dared bring that subject up with the General.

Tai asked the children about their day, and he heard with pleasure about their games and their training. But as the children were describing their exploits, Tai's gaze drifted into a preoccupied stare.

"Father? Are you alright?" Hennelyn asked suddenly. Tai quickly lifted his head and attempted to smile.

"It's all right, children. I was just thinking. I... I have some news for all of us here. But first, Jaero Lite... how did my children do in their lessons this morning?"

The tutor sniffed. "It was a warm day, sir, and so of course they had little attention for me. I could not keep them in the schoolroom for more than an hour," he reported. He spoke with annoyance, but everyone could see the slightly upturned corners of his mouth.

"After all, Jaero Lite, it will be winter in a couple of months, and then there will be plenty of dreary days for us to spend with you and your books," Arcmas assured him.

"Dreary? I hope the dreariness is not due to me!" came Jaero Lite's crestfallen answer.

"No, no!" giggled Hennelyn. "You know we like your lessons!"

"I thank you, Mistress," the tutor acknowledged with a polite inclination of the head.

"You children ought to be thankful every day that you have a teacher as wise and as knowledgeable as Jaero Lite," put in the governess. "After all, you are as well educated, or better, than any of the children in the great Starkhon houses. Now if only you, Hennelyn, could spend a little more time on your music and the finer arts, there would be no girl your like in all the northern kingdom." Her eyes riveted on Hennelyn.

"Now, Lisha, don't start! Don't forget that I am a Starkhon maiden and not like Mother. I have my horsemanship to practice, too."

"Yes, I know," Lisha allowed with a smile. "But you are already so good at that."

Hennelyn turned back to the general. "Father, what is your news that you wanted to tell us?" she reminded him.

"Oh, yes," he said vaguely. "Well, the first part of the news is that we are expecting a visit from Ambassador Siras Thraulor in a few days."

Hennelyn frowned. "He's coming again?" she said with distaste. "Haven't we been following orders well enough since last time? He was here only four months ago."

Tai huffed. "He doesn't come to make sure I am following orders, child. He knows me better than that!"

"But every time he comes, you get new orders, or need to follow old ones better, or something like that. I don't like how he talks to you, Father."

"Well, after all, Hennelyn, he is one of the emperor's most trusted ambassadors. I suppose that means he can talk any way he wishes. And it's to be expected that our emperor is interested in how we are getting on with our invasion here."

"I wish we could just leave the bunjis alone. They were here first, after all. Why should we try to conquer them?"

Somehow her father smiled and frowned at the same time.

"You sound just like your mother. Starkhons never say such things, my girl."

Hennelyn shrugged indifferently. She'd heard that speech before, but she could not help the gentler nature that she had inherited, mostly from her mother.

Tai went on, "At any rate, the ambassador isn't coming with new advice or orders this time. I received a message the day before yesterday telling me the reason for his visit." Tai dabbed at his lips with his cloth napkin and his eyes rested on Arcmas, who shifted nervously.

"He's coming for you, Arcmas."

The youngster's eyes, colored a hawk-like topaz, opened wide. His lips twitched, but no sound escaped. The others only stared.

"F-for me?" Arcmas stammered at last. "I don't understand, sir. What does he want with me?"

Tai sighed heavily.

"I should have told you this long ago, son. We've raised you ever since you were a little downy thing about two years old. But you don't really belong to us at all. You were given to us, and we were told how to raise you, with strict instructions. We were meant to give you back when you reached fifteen years of age, and, well - your birthday is next Thursday. And so we did as we were told. The years went by so fast, and it never seemed to be the right time to tell you that you would have to leave us. Your mother would have found it impossible to bear, I'm sure. Perhaps it is best that she did not live to see this day... "

Arcmas stared. In a shaky voice, he asked, "But who, sir? Who wants me back?"

Tai cleared his throat.

"The Emperor, Tol Lorsumn. It was he who sent you to us, those years ago. And now... now I must send you back."

"The emperor..." breathed Arcmas. He looked around at the other two adults. "Did you know about this?" They exchanged a nervous glance.

"Once we did. But we had forgotten it, Master Arcmas," Jaero Lite told him quietly.

Arcmas glared at Hennelyn, but she shook her head mutely. She looked stricken. Her voice hitched a bit as she asked, "But why, Father? Why does the emperor want Arcmas?"

"I don't know," Tai sighed. "It was, and still is, his command. We may all have forgotten, but apparently he hasn't. It is not our place to question the mighty Ruler of the Empire."

"Are we all moving to Starkha then, sir?" queried Arcmas.

Tai hesitated. "No. My orders here still stand. I am to remain here until I have succeeded in subduing this country, and my household stays with me. Only you are to go, Arcmas."

There was a short silence. Then everyone started talking at the same time.

"He's too young..." objected Lisha.

"His education is not finished!" added Jaero Lite. "There are years to go yet, sir."

"What about us, Father? Don't you and I get a say in it?" Hennelyn cried.

Arcmas stood up abruptly, capturing everyone's attention. "But surely, sir, you and Hennelyn may come with me! Perhaps if we ask..." He directed a wistful look at Tai. But the hope rapidly died out of his face when the general shook his head.

"No, Arcmas. The orders are specific that you go alone. We cannot disobey the emperor." Arcmas glanced around at the others. Lisha pressed her fingers against her mouth, eyes lowered. Hennelyn stared straight ahead. Only Jaero Lite met Arcmas's gaze, a look of sympathy in his blue eyes.

Arcmas stood and walked a little ways away, turning his back to them. He stood as straight and proud as any Starkhon, though his wing-tips were all quivering, betraying his emotion. Yet when he spoke, his voice was steady.

"Of course, Father. Our place is to hear and obey." He turned to face them. "When... when will the ambassador be here?"

"In three or four days. You won't be leaving immediately, I am sure. Come and sit back down, Arcmas. We can talk more about it."

Arcmas said, "No, I... think I would just like to go outside for a little while by myself. May I, sir? I won't be long." After a moment, Tai nodded. Arcmas went to the door and slipped out, closing it softly behind himself.

Whatever else the others might have said died in their throats when they looked at General Tai's set face. They knew better than to question him when he looked like that.

Dinner was over. A silence settled on the room except for the snap of the flames in the fireplace. Jaero Lite and Lisha obeyed a silent signal from their master and stood up together. They left the table and retired to their first floor rooms flanking the doorway on the south side of the hall.

After a moment, Hennelyn plucked up the courage to speak. "Father?"

"Hmm?" He looked up distractedly.

"Why does the emperor want Arcmas now? I mean, most Starkhons don't leave home to become soldiers until they are eighteen. Arcmas is only going to be fifteen."

Her father's shoulders jerked up in a slight shrug.

"Hennelyn, I don't know. Those are our orders."

"Orders," Hennelyn repeated flatly. "If Mother were here, she would have had something to say about 'orders.' And about family, and our duty to each other. If Mother were here —"

"Enough, Hennelyn!" Tai interrupted harshly. "Your mother is

11

not here! And even if she were..." He paused. When he spoke again, his voice was calmer. "I didn't mean to say it like that, child. But you know what would happen even if your mother objected to this... as we both know she would if she were here today. But as a soldier and a general... you and I know that I cannot object. No one..." He stopped.

"Yes, Father, I know. No one disobeys the emperor," Hennelyn finished bitterly. She stood and left him, climbing the staircase to the second-floor rooms where her bedchamber was situated in the west corner. Tai was left sitting alone by the fire, watching the light outside the windows fade as the rich sunset gold turned to dusk.

Up in the sky, Arcmas glided effortlessly between crimson and saffron clouds and the purpling hues of the earth below. From his vantage point, the prairie stretched out like an unending darkling carpet, and the western mountains put off their crowns of gold in favor of bald heads, sharp and black. The air was cool enough to shiver the spines of most, but Arcmas did not feel the cold. This was his element; the breeze which buoyed him felt as warm and caressing as a zephyr. He banked to the left and slid speedily on a thrilling downdraft before rising again on a warmer column of air. His wingtips spread and fluttered wildly as the wings rose, but sealed together and ballooned him upward on the downswing, all without conscious thought. Utter freedom! Off one wingtip, in perfect imitation of his maneuvers, flew his pet hawk, Glider.

His head whirled with thoughts: *Why is this happening now? What does the emperor want with me? What will he expect of me? If the emperor had me first... does he know where I come from?*

Then a sudden prompt from the deepest, loneliest corner of his soul: *Could this mean he knows where I come from?*

Of course, Arcmas had always seen that he was different from everyone else. Though he had from his earliest years flown distances that would have astonished and dismayed his adopted family if they'd known, he had never seen anyone, anywhere, who was anything like himself.

# Chapter Two

As it happened, Siras Thraulor didn't arrive before six days had gone by. The children tried to pack as much fun as they could into this time. In vain did Jaero Lite crack the books of learning for them, and in vain did their trainers try to keep them to their daily regimens. Nik, too, ducked out of chores as much as he could so that he could join his friends. At another time he would have faced punishment for such behavior, and so would Hennelyn and Arcmas, but at this particular time the adults chose to ignore it. So they made the most of this short, charmed period of time.

One day found them out riding, Hennelyn on her palomino gelding named Wingfoot, Arcmas on his black gelding he called 'Steed' (he had little imagination when it came to names), and Nik on any horse they could beg or borrow.

Another day, they spent time scrambling among the huge gnarled roots of an ancient spruce on the north side of the hill, about half a mile from the Outpost. The coulee dropped steeply down there to the creek at its bottom. The north side grew thick bush, but the south slopes were bare, the usual for this part of the country. This creek was one of the children's favorite places. They stayed out as late as they could get away with every evening, even though it was September and the days were shortening.

Wednesday dawned sunny and warm, and Hennelyn begged a picnic lunch from the kitchen workers for herself, Arcmas, and Nik. When it was ready, they took it to the sunniest part of the compound, up against the southern wall and ate it there, washing it down with clear, cold water from the creek.

Afterwards, the three of them laid down on the tough prairie grass. The sun rode high, the air was still, and it was pleasant to lie there while the heat baked them.

"Ahhh... this is the life," commented Nik, eyes shut against the glare as he lay on his back. From all around sounded the secretive *psst! psst!* of grasshoppers concealed in the long grass, still alive and unmolested by frost.

"Yes," sighed Hennelyn. "I wish winter didn't have to come at all. It seems to me that summer started only a short time ago. In winter, Father will want to hunt for the bunjis again. I don't even think there are any left around here anymore, though. They seem to be moving further and further away."

"Don't you believe it!" Nik answered. "My father says that they won't give up this land so easily. He says it's getting harder for our wagons from the east to get in and out of here, and that if we don't force an open fight with them soon, we'll all have to move away."

"And of course everyone knows that your father, the gardener from the southern lands, is an expert on battle strategy," Arcmas mocked lightly, raising up his face from where it was laying on top of his arms. A hot blush infused Nik's fair face.

"My father may be a gardener, but he's still clever!" he retorted. Arcmas relented.

"I know he is, Nik. And he's right. The bunjis have not gone away. I see them often, especially on some moonlit nights. They look for me now, though, before they move around. Still, they cannot see me as soon as I see them."

The other two nodded. Arcmas often boasted that his eyes were as sharp as any eagle's.

Hennelyn suddenly said, "I think that we Starkhons should all leave here. It's a nice place, and I think of it as home now. But I'd rather live back in Flaethe where there is not so much talk of wars and battles. And I had more friends there who were girls." She paused. "And in Glott, too, there were more girls."

"That's a woman for you!" laughed Arcmas, but Nik asked humbly, "Am I not a good enough friend for you, Henna?" She smiled at him.

"Of course you are, Nik. But just think what fun it would be if there were more of our age around! And if we didn't live in someone else's country, we could go wherever we wished without dragging guards along to spoil the fun. I'm never allowed to go far by myself."

She was silent for a time. Suddenly she sat up, her eyes glowing with mischief. Nik regarded her and groaned.

"I know that look!" he said nervously. "You're hatching a plan!"

She was staring at Arcmas's wings as they furled and unfurled from his back. He studied her in turn from his position on his stomach, his face cupped in his hands.

"I know what we should do!" she exclaimed. "Arcmas, don't you think it's been a while since you gave Nik and me a ride?"

"Oh no, I knew it," moaned Nik. "Come on, Henna, you know I get airsick! And your father doesn't like Arcmas doing that." But Arcmas started to smile.

"I think it's a good idea," he agreed. "It might be the last time we can do it before I have to leave."

"Well, I'm having no part of it," sulked Nik.

"Come on, Nik," Hennelyn chided him. "You spoilsport!"

She and Arcmas stood up. Nik did not, even when Hennelyn kicked his foot sharply.

"Alright Nik - suit yourself!" Arcmas retorted. He peered around. Only one soldier could be seen on this side of the house, accompanied by a dog on a leash. He was busy training the dog and not looking in their direction.

Arcmas boosted Hennelyn up piggy-back, his huge wings spread wide. He took a few running steps, flapping strongly. Nik stood up quickly to watch them go. The two of them rounded the corner of the house, skimming along just over the ground. But it wasn't long before Nik could see them rising high over the roof. He could hear a couple of soldiers on the other side shout and the dogs barking madly as Arcmas and Hennelyn left the compound.

Hennelyn thrilled to the joy of flight. The wind roared in her ears, and her hair streamed out behind her. The gleaming sun dazzled her eyes and made them flow with happy tears. On either side, Arcmas's strong wings beat with a hypnotic rhythm; he surged upwards as though the power of the air coursed through his veins. Arcmas had done this a few times before, and she loved it - the wonderful, wild freedom of it.

Why couldn't I have been born with wings?! she sorrowed, as she often had before. Of course, she had no sensation of the effort that it cost Arcmas to carry her, though she knew of another of his peculiarities; he was very strong - much stronger than any Starkhon boy his age. Maybe he was even stronger than a man, for all she knew.

She shook the water out of her eyes and peered down to see how high they were. Wonderfully high! On the upbeats of Arcmas's wings, she could see the walled fortress below, and the small, neat soldiers' town on the west side of it, lower down the hill. She could also see the farmers' fields, which fed everyone, stretched out on the valley floor north of the river. A few glints of reflected sunshine in them puzzled her until she realized that the farmers were likely swathing the crops with their long, horse-drawn blades. The twisty river glistened far below like a wet snake.

Arcmas flew to a hill on the south side of the valley, the wild side where no Starkhons yet lived. Here he spiralled down and put her on her feet on the scrubby grass. He turned away and spread his wings again.

"Where are you going?" she asked.

"To collect Nik," he answered. "Don't you want him here too?"

"Oh! Sure."

He took off again. Hennelyn looked around her. She stood alone on the crest of a prairie hill quite a ways southwest from the taller hill where the fortress stood, like a crown on its highest point - the place strategically chosen by her father when they first came out here. She saw no danger of any kind nearby, so she sat down to rest her legs, wobbly from the short flight, to await Arcmas's return.

It wasn't long until she saw him returning, with another burden. He was quite close before she could tell that he carried Nik in his arms, not on his back. Nik had his hands over his eyes.

Arcmas angled towards the hill, coming in low as he neared Hennelyn. He landed in a flurry of air that lifted her hair momentarily, setting Nik on his feet the same time as his own touched down. Nik finally removed his hands to see that he was down, but only Arcmas's arms around him seemed to be keeping his legs from collapsing. After a moment, he pulled away from Arcmas's loosening claws, then turned around and gave the other boy - who was in the middle of a laugh - a hefty shove. Down went Arcmas, landing on his rump with a surprised grunt and a flurry of loose feathers.

"You stupid jaybird!" Nik yelled at him. "I told you to leave me alone!"

Immediately, the fun died out of Arcmas's face, and his straight black feathery brows almost met in the middle. Then up he jumped - as quickly as he'd gone down.

"What did you call me?"

"Wendaniko!" cried Hennelyn, shocked yet hiding a smile. Nik's face flushed a blotchy red. He knew he was in trouble whenever he heard his full name, but he was too angry to care.

Hennelyn quickly moved between the two of them, holding Arcmas back.

"Come on, you two," she chided, "We didn't do this so that you could fight. You're spoiling the fun!"

"You heard what he said!" Arcmas hissed, "I am not a bird, do you hear? Not a bird!" His yellow eyes almost shot sparks. Hennelyn clung to his shirt tenaciously.

Over her shoulder, she scolded, "Nik! Why did you have to call him the one thing that makes him crazy?"

"I... I forgot," Nik lied.

"You forgot!" spat Arcmas. "Well, now you'll forget what it's like to be in one piece!"

Hennelyn decided it was time to put her foot down. In fact, she stamped it. Red-faced too now, she ordered sharply, "Arcmas! Stop it! Do you boys want to waste the last bit of time we have together fighting? Say you're sorry, Nik, and then I want both of you to make it up!"

Arcmas crossed his arms sullenly, eyeing Nik and waiting.

"Alright!" Nik offered with bad grace. "I'm sorry! I'm sorry I said... that word. I just wish that sometimes he would just - "

Hennelyn interrupted, "Well, he said he was sorry. Can you both do the secret handshake now?" Little by little, Arcmas's breathing calmed down and the anger left his face. After a moment, he stepped closer to Nik and offered his hand. Nik hesitated and searched the other boy's face.

"Friends?" he inquired cautiously.

"Friends." So they did the handshake the three of them had invented just for themselves, secret and complicated. Perhaps the boys' tempers hadn't subsided completely though, for when it was over, they both rubbed their bruised knuckles.

In the hiatus after making peace, they all finally realized that they were gloriously alone.

"Hey... we did it!" exulted Hennelyn, stretching her arms wide.

"Yes. And are we going to be in trouble!" Nik warned.

Arcmas grinned and shrugged.

"It's not an adventure if we don't get into trouble."

"Let's go explore!" cried Hennelyn, and so they did, exploring among the trees surrounding the grassy knoll. They soon tired of that, however, and a quarter of an hour later found them all sitting in a good climbing tree in comfortable silence, their friendship fully restored. The breeze dandled the leaves, and there were birds all around; chickadees said their name over and over, and above all came the lonely scree of a hawk. Arcmas's sharp eyes sought it out and watched it soar above them.

"Glider followed us. That reminds me," he mused quietly, "I will need to set him free before I go."

"Really? After you raised him from a chick?" Hennelyn asked. "Besides, he's free already. He only comes to you when you call him. Maybe he'll follow you east."

"I can't believe you'll be gone," Nik put in sadly. "Who am I going to have now, to do risky things with?" The other two laughed, since Nik with his gentle nature seldom thought up adventures.

Arcmas told him, "I'll miss you too, gardener's son. And you'll still have Hennelyn." Yet again, Nik's cheeks turned pink, but this time it was with pleasure.

Arcmas's head cocked sideways in that way he had, his hawk-yellow eyes blinking.

"I hear horses. Soldiers are coming for us," he announced. The children climbed from the tree to await them on the ground. Squinting, Hennelyn and Nik could see the tiny figures of soldiers on horseback before the trees beside the river hid them.

"Uh-oh," quavered Nik.

"Never mind, you coward," Arcmas teased him. "No one ever does anything to you. You're always the one dragged along against your will, remember?"

"We may as well walk downhill to meet them," Hennelyn said.

Closer to the river, they met up with the four men sent out after them, dripping water from fording the stream.

"Solit Ghoran," Hennelyn greeted the first.

"Mistress."

He drew up before the children with a scowl and reined in to let the man behind him approach more closely.

"And Solit Overon," she sighed. Both of these men were favored guards of her father's. She was not sure of the names of the other two soldiers behind. Overon looked her over. He was taller than Ghoran, and his hazel eyes held more intelligence. Hennelyn knew him well enough to see that he was put out, though not really that angry.

In a dry voice, he asked them, "So I suppose you children thought that was a lark, did you? Whose idea was it?" Hennelyn and Arcmas looked at one another wide-eyed and shrugged, feigning innocence.

"Er - we don't remember, sir," contributed Hennelyn.

"I see. Well, never mind. I'll leave it up to General Kanow to work out your proper punishment. In the meantime, this prank is over, and that is my decision to make. Will you ride home willingly, or shall I have to tie you to our saddles?" He spoke this lightly, but the three

18

young people were not fooled: he meant it.

Hennelyn answered humbly, "Yes, sir, we're coming."

Overon pulled Hennelyn up onto his mount behind him as though she weighed as little as one of Arcmas's feathers. Ghoran took Nik, and they headed back to the Outpost in disapproving silence. Arcmas flew back, of course, for the only horse that would carry him without fear was his own Steed.

When they arrived at the stables, the weapons-and-stable-master Solit Loroy came forward with one of his stable hands to assist with the horses. Hennelyn spotted Ghoran already striding quickly towards the house as she dismounted, and sighed again.

"Ghoran is going to tell on us," she told the other two after Arcmas landed beside them. Nik looked grim, but Arcmas shrugged. There was nothing to do about it now. They walked towards the house.

Another soldier approached them from inside. He said ominously, "Master Arcmas... Mistress Hennelyn... your father is waiting in his office to see you. You first, young mistress."

"Alright," sighed Hennelyn. She squared her shoulders and followed the guard away. As she left, one of Nik's younger brothers ran up to tell him he had chores waiting.

"And I've only been home for ten minutes," complained Nik. He turned to go, but as he did, he patted Arcmas's shoulder.

"Well... good luck," Nik said solemnly, and then walked off with his brother, an eight-year-old version of himself. Arcmas watched them go with a smile. He waited patiently until he was summoned inside.

Sometime later, Arcmas came back outside to find Hennelyn. He discovered her sitting on a rock just outside the open gate, looking north over the prairie. He squatted down beside her.

"Well, how did you do?" he asked.

"Oh, I got the usual lecture," she answered dispiritedly. "But mostly what Father wanted to tell me is that Siras Thraulor is expected to arrive this evening, and that I have to be on my best behavior from now on. Ugh!" She shivered.

Arcmas nodded dourly. Hennelyn peered more closely at his face. He seemed to be thinking grim thoughts.

"What about you? Were you punished?"

His eyes came back to her and one corner of his mouth turned up wryly.

"I thought for a minute that he was going to thrash me one last time, even though he hasn't for years. He made me promise never to fly with you again. As though you could be in any danger when I have you! But we talked mostly about Ambassador Thraulor, too, and about my leaving here."

Hennelyn sighed. "It's happening too fast," she murmured. "And now that awful Siras Thraulor is going to be here on your birthday. What rotten luck!"

"Well, I'm not going to let it ruin my 'coming of age' party," Arcmas remarked firmly.

"That's the spirit!" exclaimed Hennelyn, cheering up. "Just wait until you see my present!" Arcmas's amber eyes peered into her sky-blue ones curiously.

"What? What is it?"

"Oh, I'm not going to tell you! It's a surprise!" she giggled, getting up and skipping mischievously away. He came after her, begging, "Come on, Henna! Just give me a hint!"

But she ran off with Arcmas following as best as he could on his slow feet, and the afternoon sun smiled down on their laughter.

# Chapter Three

Siras Thraulor, Ambassador of Emperor Tol Lorsumn, did indeed arrive late that evening. So late, in fact, that Hennelyn and Arcmas were in their bedrooms asleep. Arcmas, however, woke to the commotion outside. He flew out through his window and balanced on the top of the house to observe the activity below.

It appeared that Siras Thraulor had come with no less than one hundred mounted soldiers, a full squadron. Arcmas wondered where they would all sleep. Then he saw them pitching tents that ballooned out and soon glowed with light from within.

He didn't watch for very long; he didn't want to think about pitching his own tent like that in a few days' time, surrounded by strangers. As he drifted down towards his bedroom, he noticed that Hennelyn's window was open, a small square of light. So she, too, had been awakened. He changed course towards her.

Hennelyn moved back from the window to let him in. She'd made a small fire in the fireplace for warmth and also lit a rush candle. Her room and Arcmas's were the only two upper bedchambers with their own fireplaces, on opposite ends of the second floor. Her chamber was not large, and the furniture in it had been hastily built from spruce or poplar wood. She had only her bed, strewn with rabbit furs, a straw tick in a wooden bed frame, a chair with seat and back woven out of branches, a chest for her clothes, and a small rickety table beside her bed on which the candle stood.

Arcmas folded up his wings and climbed in through the small opening with some difficulty.

"You heard them arrive?" he asked. She nodded. They both sat down on her bed.

"It sounds like a lot of them this time," Hennelyn guessed.

"Yes... a whole squadron."

Hennelyn reached out a comforting hand and touched the soft, cool feathers of his arm. He was wearing only night breeches.

"Are you nervous?" she asked. He looked at her and gave a forced smile, admiring the way the candle flame gilded her hair and turned her blue eyes to aquamarine.

"I'll be fine," he answered stoutly. "Father's right, it is an honor to be called by the great Tol Lorsumn. And I'm not a child anymore. If other recruits can leave their families to complete their training, then so can I. Most of them are only three years older than I am."

"They are all at least eighteen," contradicted Hennelyn.

"Well... I'll be fifteen tomorrow."

"Yes... but that's still young. You ought to stay with your family for now..." She folded her arms in annoyance. "But that's against orders!"

Arcmas's mouth still smiled, but into his yellow eyes crept that lost look that she recognized only too well, and she spoke to reassure him, "We are your family, Arcmas."

"But we've always known that I was adopted. I mean... look at me."

Hennelyn answered stubbornly, "Mother always said it didn't matter what you looked like, that you were meant to be part of us." She reached out and picked up his hand. It was bigger than hers, tipped with razor-sharp claws, but it was the hand of her brother, and she did not fear it. Never in her memory had he ever been anything but gentle with her. He curved his leathery fingers round hers, squeezing slightly.

"How do you remember Mother so well? We were only seven when she died," he mused.

"I will never forget Mother," she answered firmly. "And neither will you,"

"Yes... you're right. But I've been thinking. I think I... I want to go. I want to meet the emperor."

Hennelyn nodded.

"Yes, I know. You'd go so that Father wouldn't get into trouble."

Arcmas eyes shifted away from hers.

"Well, yes, I guess so. Though that's not the reason I'm thinking of."

"But why else?"

"Because, Henna, because!" He let go of her hand and bounced up off of the bed. "Don't you understand? The Emperor gave me to you. That means he knows where I really came from! Now do you see?"

She said nothing.

He went on earnestly, "All my life, I've wanted to know where I came from. I've wanted to know... are there others like me? And now... here is someone who can tell me! I have to ask him, Henna!" Arcmas

22

stopped, sitting down rigidly. His next words were barely audible. "I've got to know," he said.

Hennelyn didn't reply. This was not something that had occurred to her, nor could she argue against it.

Arcmas reached out and lifted her chin so that she looked at him. He teased, "Don't worry. I'll come back again, no matter what. You and Nik won't have too much fun without me, will you?" She rolled her eyes, trying to hide her tears.

"Oh... I guess there'll be time for the three of us to have fun before you go away. And you never know, maybe Father and I will be able to come after all." Arcmas didn't contradict her. He grinned instead.

"Maybe. We'd sure have fun in the capital city. We haven't been to a big city for ages. Well, I'd better get back to bed. I'll even try to sleep - if I can!"

"Yeah. Until tomorrow, then. Goodnight, Arcmas."

"Goodnight, Henna." Instead of flying out of the window again, he chose to walk through her door to his own room at the other end of the walkway, treading carefully on his clawed feet. Hennelyn blew out her candle and laid down, but she stayed awake a long time.

The next day, the morning of Arcmas's fifteenth birthday, dawned clear and warm again. All of the household had a part to play in the important occasion. The extra staff recruited from the farms were up cooking and baking all sorts of special dishes already; pails of berries sat on the counters, and flour dust drifted everywhere.

Arcmas came down to breakfast a little late because of last night's disturbed slumber. As he stepped down the wide staircase, he saw that General Kanow, Hennelyn, and the ambassador were already seated at the table. Jaero Lite and Lisha rarely ate with them when Siras was there; he disapproved of 'servants' eating with the family. The kitchen workers were serving a larger, fancier breakfast than usual to please the guest.

As Arcmas reached the bottom of the stairs, Tai said, "Ah, Your Excellency, here is the boy now."

He stood up and impatiently waved the youth over.

"Come, Arcmas, the ambassador awaits you."

At that, the man sitting with his back to the stairs also stood and turned slowly, revealing to Arcmas the thin, sharply planed face of Siras Thraulor. He was in full uniform but for the helmet, and over that was draped a rich robe of deep black lined inside with scarlet. His short hair was steely grey, scraped back over his skull. His hair matched his eyes, which fastened onto Arcmas immediately. Unlike most Starkhons, he had no beard or mustache. His thin lips split into a humorless smile in greeting; even his teeth seemed greyish.

Hesitating only slightly, Arcmas came purposefully forward, stopping to salute in the proper way, bowing slightly at the waist, his right arm at an angle across his chest.

"Your Excellency," Arcmas greeted him politely.

"Ah, Arcmas, my boy. We meet again," returned Siras. His voice did not fit his granite appearance. It was soft, cultured and smooth.

"Yes, sir."

"Are you looking forward to your new life as a soldier?"

Arcmas felt exposed before that penetrating gaze.

"Of course, sir."

"Yes... after all, you're fifteen now. No longer a child. It's time for you to get out into the civilized world and discover what you are capable of. Come, sit down, boy."

Since the ambassador sat in Hennelyn's usual place, and she'd moved next to Arcmas's stool, Arcmas walked around and sat down beside Hennelyn. The servants busied themselves filling Arcmas's plate. With his eyes partly lidded, Siras watched the two children smile nervously at each other, a twitch hardly more than the compression of their lips.

Tai ventured, "Of course you know, Your Excellency, that you and your escort are invited to Arcmas's coming of age celebrations today?"

"Thank you, General, I will let my aide know. I believe I will only be bringing my Centenors and the Decenors. There are two or three among them who will be part of Arcmas's new training program. They will be interested in seeing how he performs today. I expect that you will make a good showing, Arcmas?"

"Yes, sir," the boy answered a little doubtfully. He was, on the whole, fairly confident in his abilities, but Siras's scrutiny would make it more difficult. Siras Thraulor had visited their family at least every couple of years ever since Arcmas could remember, and it was always with the effect of making him feel like he was on trial. At least now he understood why Siras had always singled him out; it was because he had been reporting on the boy to his own superiors. Siras seemed less than pleased with Arcmas's lukewarm answer, replying, "Yes... well, if there are any weak points left in you, the officers will know how to get rid of them, I am sure."

Arcmas's eyes fell, and Hennelyn noticed the spots of color high on his cheeks. She understood how he felt; the ambassador had much the same effect on her.

Breakfast went on with Tai and Siras lapsing into discussion about the successful forays into bunji territory, and the annoyance they had been to the Outpost since Siras was last there.

Tai explained, "You see, sir, a common bunji strategy is to lay traps along caravan routes and loot the goods in the confusion. Since there are hundreds of prairie miles to travel, it's nearly impossible for the Starkhons to anticipate them, and therefore impossible to plan for. A few bunjis have been killed in these attacks, but none captured. The bunji campaigns are more mischievous than violent."

"Violent?" Siras echoed. "Of course they are not violent. Over the past forty years, since we first discovered the vermin, we have never found these bunjis to be violent. Their..." his lip curled over the word, "...faith... prohibits violence. They will only try to defend themselves when pressed, even though they are no match for us. But we have discovered in the years we've spent invading this land that all you need to do, General Kanow, is capture one bunji here. That will lead to finding their local leader, their 'Laero,' or 'Laera,' as the case may be.

"When you have your hands on that one, then you get them to give up their 'Adon Miru,' their spiritual leader. You kill that one and then the game is over - this new territory will be ours. Those bunjis who do not assimilate and worship our emperor will be imprisoned or eliminated. It has worked this way in the past with all the bunji territories we have overtaken. I am sure you will find that it will work here, too."

"Your Excellency!" protested the general, his eyes on the children. Siras made an impatient gesture.

"This is pointless conversation. You have been fully briefed on all of this. And these two youngsters ought to know how our empire works by now. Have they not been taught about our glorious history - conquering all who stand against us?"

"Of course, Excellency," conceded Kanow. But his quick glance at his children warned them to betray nothing by their faces. None too soon, because Siras also glanced at them sharply.

Siras continued, "And here you have been sitting, for almost two years; a general like you who should be commanding an entire touman of men — ten thousand men, General! But you are stuck out at this outpost with a mere two hundred soldiers, still searching for the elusive local populace."

"With all due respect, your Excellency, you must realize that the first year was spent on building, settling, and starting farms here. This is a wild country. The winters are long and cold."

Siras shrugged contemptuously. "Yes, yes. I have spent a winter or two in this area. You forget that I have been stationed in Khuntz the last couple of years – only two weeks' travel east of here. In fact, that is partly why Emperor Tol Lorsumn has asked that Arcmas here be trained early. To solve this impasse."

"You've been living in Khuntz?" Tai asked in surprise. "You must have moved there right after we left. I ask your pardon, sir, but what can Arcmas do about this? We have tried finding the bunjis even with dogs, but they can't seem to help us. We were not lucky enough to find these locals just sitting in villages, waiting for us to arrive as the first ones did years ago. They are actively hiding. And fighting back, in their fashion."

"And yet Arcmas has seen them, hasn't he?"

There came a pause in which these words revolved slowly through the great room. Then Siras added with significance, "If he can see them, he can catch them."

Tai objected, "Sir, Arcmas is not a soldier; he is still a child. We don't expect him to–"

"And that," interrupted Siras, "is why I am here, General. The emperor always wanted to train Arcmas for military action like most other Starkhon boys. But when we return him in a few months, he will be especially useful to us in solving the bunji problem here. And eventually even further west. You must see, from his unique capabilities, that he will be the best arrow in our entire quiver for this hide and seek business! This is the will of the Emperor."

Tai's face had been hardening as Siras spoke, and now it was set like a flint about to spark. But the flame did not break out.

Instead, he commanded shortly, "Children, if you are finished eating, it's time to start your preparations for today. Go on now - as long as the Ambassador does not object?"

Siras seemed about to speak, but then sat back in his chair instead, eyes on Tai.

"Yes, yes… you are dismissed, children," Siras said, again with a languid flap of the hand. The servants arrived to pick up the dishes and remove uneaten food.

When she knew it was impossible to be overheard over the

clatter of plates, Hennelyn waited for Arcmas to catch up to her further down the room. She made a face, and hissed, "What an awful breakfast! I wish that he didn't have to eat with us all the time. At least now we know what he expects of you."

"Do we?" Arcmas murmured. He shook himself; and his wings half-unfurled from their tight fit against his body. He continued, "Well, I guess we will see. But I don't want to think about it now. I have better things to think of. It's my birthday, remember?"

Shortly after lunch hour, the festivities began.

As guests, the marshal came with his family, the two centenors with theirs, and all of the twenty decenors. Arcmas's trainer Echthus was there and Ghundrew, too. Those who had wives and older children brought them, but the number of single soldiers greatly outweighed that of the married ones.

There were a few other youngsters in their teens there, mostly the three sons and daughter of Marshal Maraton and the two children of Centenor Stankhreed, a boy and a girl, as well as Centenor Hernak's eldest daughter. The boys attending were all older than Arcmas by two or three years.

The guests did not bring gifts; only the family of the one coming of age did. In the end, Siras Thraulor came with only three others: his aide Hanthor, his own Marshal Stokhor, and Centenor Jakhron. His other men stayed near their tents inside the compound.

Arcmas looked very grown up in his burgundy dress uniform as he welcomed people alongside General Kanow. A flurry of military salutes broke out around the hall as the soldiers greeted those of higher rank and bowed over the hands of the ladies.

For once, Hennelyn wore a gown which fell down to her ankles and had let her maid Dewdra sculpt her unruly hair into shining braids that wound around her head. The startling transformation from tomboy to lady drew the eyes of many young males there.

When everyone had arrived, Arcmas and the other teens put on their leather training gear, and they all moved outside. The walled enclosure of prairie grass would serve as the arena for the games, which were really a contest of skills between Arcmas and the other teenage boys there - those who had already had their coming of age and were training as soldiers. This part of the celebration was for Arcmas to prove himself a man.

There were swordplay matches, archery matches, armed charges on horseback, and a little bit of hand-to-hand combat. Arcmas did well enough in most things. He was quick and strong despite his slender build. But he was not nearly as good at archery as Hennelyn was. It was not that he didn't practice; it was because his clawed hands were always getting hooked or slicing the bowstrings.

Where he really shone was in fighting with a cuilla. His trainer Decenor Echthus knew this, and had saved these matches for last. The cuilla is a long metal staff. The real ones had a sharp retractable blade on either end, but today these had been removed. The games were meant merely to entertain - the ends of the staff were on this occasion coated with yellow powder. The goal was to jab the opponent's body with one blunt end of the staff as close to the heart as possible, and the resulting powder mark would determine the winner.

Of course, it was especially difficult to fight someone who could fly out of the way or attack from above, and Arcmas was not ashamed to use this to his advantage. One by one he defeated the other young men. The general audience cheered Arcmas's wins dutifully - most of them probably thinking Arcmas's special skills were totally unfair. But the staff of the Outpost made up for their lack of enthusiasm. Everyone could hear young Nik's loud hurrahs. Then Decenor Echthus stepped up as an opponent.

Everyone was surprised, but the decenor and Arcmas had planned this together. At first, they scowled at each other in the best Starkhon tradition, but it didn't last long; a slow smile crept over both faces. It was easy to see that Echthus, at least, was truly fond of his strange pupil. They grasped their cuillas in both hands and fell into fighting stance.

First came the slow circling, sizing each other up. Then they each made a feint or two in the other's direction, neither making anycontact. Arcmas attacked first. He brought his cuilla up high and then slashed it downwards with all his strength. But Echthus was ready. He took the blow with the middle of his own staff, holding it between his hands. The metal staffs rang as they connected, slowly at first, then faster and faster.

It was like sword-fighting except that a cuilla is longer and can be grasped anywhere along its length. Arcmas's other opponents had fought him almost half-heartedly, waiting for him to use his unfair advantages; but Echthus knew every trick, and he wasn't letting Arcmas off easy.

The cuillas spun around in their hands like juggler's props, glinting in the afternoon sun. The audience hardly dared to blink for fear of missing a move. Arcmas was up, then down, his wings flashing - sparks flying from the cuillas as they clashed.

Suddenly Arcmas was on the defensive. He spun away from Echthus, trying to create space, switching his hands for an offensive move. As he turned, ready to attack, Echthus planted his cuilla on the ground in front of him, holding it vertically at arm's length to signal the end of the mock battle.

"Stop!" he shouted, panting. "I've marked you, Arcmas!"

Arcmas stared at him with astonishment, breathing hard. "You haven't!"

Echthus grinned. "Yes I have, boy. Look at your back." Arcmas swiveled, spreading his loosely folded wings apart, and craned his head over his shoulder to look. Sure enough, there was a yellow splotch on his tunic just beside his left wing.

"You're right!" he cried with a laugh. "Today you got the better of me, Echthus."

He clapped his trainer on the arm. Everyone cheered, released from their tension by this final blow. Even Siras Thraulor's colorless eyes glittered with pleasure.

After the games, everyone moved back into the hall for the feast. Arcmas had to wash up and put his dress uniform back on, and they waited until he was present before starting. As Arcmas was a general's son, even an adopted one, there were decorations, drinks, and delicacies that most birthday parties went without. Tai had even supplied zorkhta from his own personal stash – a strong alcoholic drink made from corn mash. Rarely seen in this isolated outpost. There was plenty to eat, and this time, there was no lack of sweet dishes. The sugar for the baked goods and other dishes had come with Siras Thraulor's convoy.

The guests moved about the many rough-hewn tables, sampling the delicious food and visiting. There were two roasted haunches of beef, small potatoes and onions in butter, many different kinds of bread from fine white loaves to heavily seeded whole grain, corn on the cob, creamed corn, cooked peas, steamed beans, as well as all of the root vegetables that could be grown over a summer and prepared in many different ways, from baked to boiled to pickled. There were cobblers made of the sweet summer berries and the sour native apples. For those who were not allowed zorkhta - which was reserved for the officers – there were berry wines and cordials, and hot spiced wild raspberry cider.

No one would go home unsatisfied.

A few soldiers turned into musicians for the night and played background melodies to liven the proceedings. When the family sat down together at the head table, everyone else followed suit, finding their seats among the many tables. The two Luinians, Lisha and Jaero Lite, were included at the head table that evening. They looked out of place among the roomful of sturdy, ebony-haired Starkhons.

At the appropriate moment, Tai stood up. This was enough to command everyone's attention. The hall fell into expectant silence. Tai's voice reached all the corners of the large space. As night fell, hundreds of candles were being lit all about the room. Nik's little brother carefully lit the ones in the two large chandeliers hanging from the ceiling, using a comically long pole with a candle on the end. The warm glow above sharpened the shadows on General Tai's face.

"Friends and fellow soldiers," Tai began, "I would like to thank you all for attending the coming of age of my son and ward, Arcmas. Today marks the end of his childhood and the beginning of his journey into manhood. I know you wish him, as much as I do, a great future as a soldier of the Empire. Let us make it official." He lifted his glass, and there was a ripple through the room as all the guests did the same. All eyes looked to Arcmas and the hall rang with their toast, "Great courage and many conquests, Arcmas!"

The clinking of glasses filled the room, then everyone threw back their heads to drink deeply.

Swallowing his cider, Arcmas stood up and spoke the appropriate reply, "From this day forward, as the emperor's soldier, I do swear to spend my life in obedience to him - for the greater honor of Tol Lorsumn and the Starkhon Empire. To the emperor!"

"To the emperor!" echoed all of the guests, and they quaffed again while the musicians played their lively national anthem. Most joined their voices to the music and sang the words as well, holding the military salute. It was a fierce, warlike song written for a conquering people, for the glory of a divine sovereign. If some happened to be slurring the words, it only testified to the excellence of the zorkhta. When that was over, the guests cheered, and Arcmas went on to thank all of them for attending, starting with his father, and all of the people who had had a hand in raising and training him up to this special day.

Last of all, he indicated Siras seated at his right and said, "I would also like to humbly thank His Excellency, the emperor's ambassador, Siras Thraulor, for coming himself to accompany me to

Starkha, where my training will be completed. I am honored, Your Excellency. Shall we all drink to the ambassador?"

"To the ambassador!" cried everyone, and Siras stood a moment to incline his head in satisfaction.

Now it was time for Arcmas to receive his gifts. The Outpost household presented him with newly-tailored clothing to take with him, the gear that he would need, and his field uniform and armor, which were of brown leather and much plainer than his dress clothes. Since General Kanow had the means to afford the best, the sword and gear that he received was of the finest make and temper, somehow ordered and spirited out to the outpost during the past few months. He was going to be one well-turned-out soldier when he got to his training base, better equipped than most Starkhons could manage.

Jaero Lite and Lisha together gave him a journal to write his new adventures in. But these, as fine as they were, were not the best of his gifts. When all this had been received and admired by Arcmas, he found that Tai had reserved something even more wonderful.

As they stood before everyone, the general reached into the wide belt of his dress uniform and brought out his own personal cuilla, fully armed and deadly when the blades were extended. In its folded form, it was like a silver tube six inches long and one inch in diameter. On one end there was a smooth ruby which, as Tai pressed it, telescoped the cuilla out to its five foot length, startling those seated nearest. The sapphire on the other end caused the closed ends of the tubes to rotate backward to present the dangerous double blades. Tai presented this to Arcmas along with its tooled case of fine leather.

Arcmas stared at it, astonished. Expensive cuillas such as these were usually handed down within a family, and this particular one had belonged to Tai's father and grandfather.

"Go on, take it, my boy," Tai urged.

"But sir! This is a Kanow heirloom, to be given to your own son or grandson someday."

Tai smiled, "I know that, Arcmas. Why do you suppose I am giving it to you?" Then his face grew solemn. "I know it's true that you ultimately belong to the emperor, but I cannot deny that you have been like a son to me all these years - a good son, and the only one I have. I want you to have this."

Arcmas could not resist these sentiments, so unlike the stern man he knew as his father. The boy took it shyly, yellow eyes aglow. He gazed at the shiny surface and the bright gems. The metal was light and supple but strong, and it gleamed a smoky silver. Silver was in its alloy, along with many other metals. Its makeup was a secret formula known only to its particular cuillasmith, a man greatly admired for his skill. Only the wealthy could afford the items of deadly art created by the great Kranokh.

So entranced was Arcmas with this gift that he did not notice the disapproving glare of Siras. The boy's attention was all for the man who had been the mainstay of his life, even if that same man had been often remote and private.

"Thank you... Father," Arcmas quietly answered, hesitating over the epithet he rarely used. They shook hands after Arcmas had folded the cuilla away into its pouch. Everyone clapped and cheered. All, that is, but Siras.

Last but not least, Hennelyn came forward with her gift. She had worked their family crest with many-colored thread onto a piece of black leather and made a pendant out of it so that it could be hung around Arcmas's neck. The Kanow crest featured a symmetrical raven with half open wings, clutching a cuilla in its two feet. It was an excellent copy of the one which Tai owned, though his was pewter and sported a few small but precious stones. Hennelyn's version was a complicated and admirable piece of work. As Arcmas pulled it on over his head, she told him softly, "It's so you don't forget us!"

"I could never do that," he returned quietly.

With that, the gift-giving was over, and the guests were free to while away the evening with song and dance and drink. The few couples got up to dance to the music, and the smaller Luinian children ran around the edges. Arcmas, Hennelyn, and Tai left their places and mingled with the guests, as did the others at the head table. But as Hennelyn moved around the room, she kept her eyes on her brother. There was one last thing that would be done tonight, and it was not a custom that she liked to contemplate. It was called 'Initiation.'

Hennelyn watched as four of the bigger youths came up behind him, one laying a hand on his arm. The smallest of them was a head taller than he. Arcmas looked around at them with solemn comprehension. He nodded at their words and walked away with them willingly enough, through the hall and out into the dark evening.

Hennelyn followed at a distance, as far as the door. As they melted into the night, she stopped in the doorway and turned back, closing the door behind her. Someone had followed her; Hennelyn looked up into the face of her father.

He smiled and said, "Never mind, Henna. He'll be alright. He is going to be a favorite of the emperor, after all, and those brash young fellows know it."

He put an arm on her shoulders and steered her back into the milling crowd, though his words did little to comfort her. She moved to the buffet table for something to drink, noticing that Siras was standing in a small group at the other end. The others with him were his aide Hanthor, a short plump man with a superior lift to his double chin, and Centenor Jakhron, who had barely left the ambassador's side all night. Siras addressed himself to these three grimly, not realizing that Hennelyn was near enough to overhear.

"I tell you, the faster we get him away, the better. I always told the emperor that it would have been best to raise the creature himself, or at least to move him from house to house, so that he would not put down any roots."

"Well, it did seem, did it not, that after the general's wife died, it had succeeded in driving a wedge between the boy and the others?" the centenor pointed out.

"Between Kanow and the boy, perhaps, but it was the girl who held them together. She has too much of her Luinian mother in her. This Arcmas creature is not as ruthless as I would like to see him." His steely gaze rested on Jakhron as he added, "Centenor, toughening the boy will be your task. We want him loyal, and as cold as ice. You will be his primary influence from now on, as his training centenor."

Jakhron saluted and bowed crisply. "It will be done, Your Excellency."

Jakhron was a tall, broad-shouldered man with a face that looked like it was blasted out of stone, and hands as big as dinner plates - a good candidate for such a job. Hennelyn shivered and moved out of earshot, troubled over what she'd heard.

A long while later, people began to drift away, taking polite leave of Tai Kanow and Hennelyn. Only those whose young men were out with Arcmas stayed behind, waiting for their sons to return. It did not take long. They were soon back, tousled and panting. Arcmas wasn't with them as expected, but when interrogated, the youths' story was that he had flown straight to the window of his room.

"And," asked the wife of Centenor Stankhreed and mother of Donotar, the eldest of the group at nineteen years, "is he a man now?" Donotar seemed oddly out of breath and not as smug as she had expected.

"Oh, indeed!" he agreed. "He's a man." He glanced covertly at the other youths, but the adults did not pry further, though they seemed puzzled. They all said their goodnights and dispersed, thanking General Kanow for the evening.

What on earth did they do? Hennelyn wondered. As the guests filtered away, she snuck upstairs to look for Arcmas.

She came to the door of his room and knocked on it. From within came his muffled, "Who is it?" but instead of answering, she pushed open the door and went straight in.

She had caught him in the act of preening his feathers in front of the warm fire, clad in nothing but plumage. In spite of the fact that Arcmas hated to be thought of as avian, Hennelyn had caught him at this before, secretly preening himself as any other bird did by instinct, keeping the feathers clean and honed for flight.

Startled, Arcmas gave a yell and dove into hiding behind his bed. From the post of the rough footboard he yanked down his back-slit robe - tailored specifically for his wings to fit through - and threw it over himself.

"What are *you* doing here?" he demanded.

For an answer, she carefully looked him over.

"You don't look hurt," she concluded with relief.

"Of course I'm not hurt!" he snorted rudely.

His dress uniform was carefully draped over a nearby chair. She reached out to stroke a sleeve.

"It's wet!" she exclaimed. She stepped closer and touched the curve of his nearest wing, and added, "You're wet, too! What happened?"

He sighed with exasperation.

"Henna, go back to your own room. Starkhon women don't ask about initiation, you know that."

"I am only half Starkhon," she replied stubbornly.

"Don't tell me - I know it too well!"

"So you don't... want to talk about it?"

His only reply was a dark look and a toss of his head. He turned his back on her and went back to warming by the fire as though she were not there. She only sat silently, waiting.

After a moment, he snapped, "If you must know - they threw me down the old well! The one we tried to dig when we first got here. There's still a little water in the bottom."

"They didn't! And they pulled the cover off and everything just for that? Were you afraid?" He turned to face her.

"Yes. You know I hate spaces too small to fly out of.

"Did they pull you up again?" He sniffed and held up his strange hand for her observation.

"I climbed out. That's what these claws are good for. Besides, there was still a piece of old rope hanging down inside it. You should have seen them run! I dive-bombed them a few times, knocked them down, but I was careful not to draw any blood."

His yellow eyes glinted with devilish glee, and the expression on his face… she gave an involuntary shiver, imagining what it must have been like for those young fellows to see him crawl dripping out of the well in the moon-ruled twilight. To see the giant shadowy wings slowly stretch wide, and after that to lose sight of him in the sky, hearing nothing but wingbeats, driven to run in front of Arcmas's inescapable fury.

"Don't tell anyone else," Arcmas cautioned. "Those boys and I don't like each other, but there's no reason to dishonor them. They'll tell their version of what happened and no one has to know that I scared them more than they scared me!"

Hennelyn nodded in agreement, smiling behind a hand.

"We'd better tell someone to put the cover on the well again,"she remarked. Arcmas nodded, with an answering grin.

"I'll tell Father tomorrow. Now get out of my room. I'm turning in; I'm tired. Goodnight, Hennelyn."

She stood, and walked to the door.

"Goodnight, Arcmas. Sleep well." She slipped out and shut the door behind her. She felt proud, reassured, but somewhat uneasy all at the same time. She'd heard a lot of strange things today. She especially wondered about Siras's words: Arcmas is not as ruthless as I would like to see him.

As she made her way along the balcony, she saw that her father's closed chamber door was edged with light. So he was still awake. But he had not bothered to check on Arcmas.

# Chapter Four

No sooner had Hennelyn sat down to breakfast the next morning when the Ambassador announced, "General Kanow, I ought to tell you that I have decided to leave for Khuntz today, as soon as all is ready. I would appreciate it if Arcmas packed immediately; it will only take a few hours for my company to be ready to travel. We have a long journey ahead of us."

Alarmed glances flashed between the other three at the table.

"A few hours, Your Excellency?" Tai stammered. "But sir, it will take me much of that time to prepare my report for the emperor. I thought that in two or three days-"

"Two or three days will be impossible," interrupted Siras. "My company and I have traveled at too easy a pace to get here, and now we shall need to make up for lost time. I would like to arrive back at Khuntz while it is still warm outside. Arcmas and I will be going on to Glott. I would like to avoid waking covered in frost if possible."

"Yes, of course, Excellency. I understand," Tai agreed doubtfully. "In that case I shall have to confine most of the inventory to estimates."

"That will do. And Arcmas," Siras went on, "I would like you to report to me as soon as possible. You have not spoken to your new trainer yet; I would like him to explain your regimen and what is to be expected of you during the journey. Every man has his job to do in my squadron, and so will you. No Starkhon soldier is without a post, even when traveling is the order of the day."

"Yes, Your Excellency-" Arcmas stopped in confusion, having risen halfway to his feet. Then he dropped down again onto his stool. He seemed evenly divided between excitement and dismay.

Siras went on, "I beg your pardons, General Kanow, and young Mistress Hennelyn. I'm afraid there won't be time for long goodbyes."

*He sounds more pleased about it than not,* Hennelyn thought darkly.

Siras's rush set the pace for the whole day. Lisha, Dewdra, and Hennelyn quickly helped Arcmas gather his things together, packing them into big saddle bags for Steed to carry. When the luggage was ready, it was taken down to the stables.

Wendaniko was helping his father and two brothers in the small flower beds, something Nik's father had not been able to resist trying out in this new place. Some plants were still blooming. It had dawned a cool and cloudy day, and everyone had put on extra layers. Nik was doing wheelbarrow duty when Hennelyn found him.

"Nik!" she cried, running up to him. All of his family ducked their heads to her respectfully, but she took no notice, chattering on breathlessly, "Nik, Arcmas is leaving today! The ambassador wants to leave before lunch, and - and he won't even let Arcmas say goodbye to anyone. You'd better come right away if you want to talk to him at all before he's gone."

Nik's face fell in dismay. His father Follamo exclaimed, "Leaving right away, young mistress! Is it truly so? Ah, it's a shame. What does the general say to that?"

"What can he say?" she replied with a shrug. "What can anyone say? What the ambassador wants, the ambassador gets. He wants to take Arcmas from us as quickly as he can. But I'm not going to let him!" She lifted a defiant chin.

Nik began to say, "But Henna-" when he caught his father's glare and changed it: "But Mistress Hennelyn, what will you do?"

She smiled mysteriously. "Come with me and I'll show you." Nik looked to his father.

"All right! Go on, son," Follamo allowed with a grin. Nik followed close on Hennelyn's heels as she turned and ran off.

As they neared the stables, they saw that Arcmas was there, supervising the loading of a mule. He was also saddling his horse, Steed. He had changed into his field uniform but had chosen only the light leather jacket to wear over it, and he had his helmet on, too, making him look very different. It was rather like a tight skullcap, except that the sides and back swooped down low to cover the entire head and most of the neck. The dull, darksome metal seemed to draw the sunlight into itself rather than reflect it.

The mule was being packed up with Arcmas's fur-lined winter jacket and brand new body armor - a long tunic with iron rings sewn into the lining. Soldiers only wore this in battle or training, as they were quite heavy to move around in.

Hennelyn and Nik ran up to him, breathless.

"Arcmas!"

Arcmas turned around to them. His solemn face lit with a smile. "Hello, you two! You've come to see me off!"

"Yes, of course. Don't you look like a soldier today?" Nik said, looking him over.

"I might look like a soldier, but I don't feel like one. I wish we weren't in such a rush. Henna, have you seen the general yet?"

"He's still making up his report, I think. This isn't fair! Why does Siras Thraulor have to leave today?" she wailed.

Nik looked shocked.

"Shouldn't you be calling him His Excellency?" he wondered.

But Hennelyn pouted, "Oh, what for? I don't think he's so 'excellent.'"

Arcmas curled an arm around Nik's slim shoulders.

"I'm glad I'll get to talk to you a bit, Nik. I wasn't able to yesterday, at the party. There were too many people around."

"Yes, I know. And I had something to give you, too, for your coming of age. I have it with me right now, actually." He hitched up his tunic a little to reach into his pants pocket, and shyly brought something out in his closed hand.

"I made it myself," he admitted, as his cheeks bloomed pink. Arcmas held out a hand, and Nik dropped into it a small horse head carved out of diamond willow wood and polished smooth.

"It's supposed to look like Steed," Nik explained.

"Hey, this is great! Look at this, Henna!" Arcmas held it up so that she could see it. It was about three inches long, a wooden portrait of a horse.

"I think it does look like Steed!" she agreed. Arcmas turned it around to see it from all angles. At last he said quietly, "Thanks, Nik. I really like it. I've always liked your carvings, but this is the best one you've done so far, I think."

Nik tried hard to shrug off the compliment, but his eyes glowed. Arcmas pretended to show Steed his likeness, stroking the gelding's mane. Steed was the only horse never to show fear of him because Arcmas had been careful to imprint himself on the animal as a newborn foal.

Arcmas added, "And did you see what Henna made me?" He reached down inside the square neck of his uniform to bring out the pendant that Hennelyn had worked so hard on.

"Yes, she showed it to me before she gave it to you. It's great," Nik agreed.

"Yeah. It sure will remind me of home to have these things with me. I'm going to guard them with my life!" It was an awkward attempt at a joke.

Then a silence thumped down between them like a heavy curtain, wrapping up in its folds many lonely thoughts that went unsaid. The soldiers talked and bustled around them, as Arcmas continued to stroke Steed's neck absentmindedly.

After a moment, Nik said sadly, "But what will we have to remember you by?"

Arcmas clapped a hand to his helmeted head. "You're right! What on earth can I give to you two?"

Henna was inclined to say that she had no need for such a thing as she was not likely to forget her own brother when Nik surprised her by making a suggestion.

"I know! How about one of your feathers? I've - I've always liked those big ones in your wings."

He was immediately embarrassed, and the hot blush, so recently faded, returned in all its glory. Arcmas was taken aback and gave a short laugh.

"But Nik, I fly with those!" Nik said nothing. Arcmas added quickly, "Oh, all right!" Then, as Nik reached out, "Oh, no, you don't! I'll get it myself!"

He didn't unfurl a wing though, but instead reached behind himself, a bit lower down than expected. He bent forward a bit, gave a wriggle and a grunt, and finally presented two feathers of about twenty-four inches in length.

"Here!" he said, presenting them to Nik and Hennelyn. "I can better spare the tail-feathers. Ow, that hurts! If I'd known that was what you wanted, I would have saved you some of those that fall off by themselves!" He was teasing, but Nik was too distracted with his gift to pay attention.

"Wow!" Nik spun the feather, watching the sun make iridescent rainbows in the darkest chocolate bands of color. Hennelyn laughed at him, though she was just as pleased with her own feather. Nik seized Arcmas's hand for the secret handshake.

They were having a good time when up strutted Siras's aid Hanthor, dampening the mood as effectively as a dark cloud blotting out the sun. He looked even smaller and rounder in a heavy black knee-length coat. His supercilious voice broke through theirs, nasal and high."Good day, young Master Arcmas and Mistress Hennelyn." He looked through Nik as though he were not there.

The other two responded in kind. When they had finished greeting him, Hanthor went on, "Arcmas, I have someone here with me who requires your attention. Your new trainer awaits you." He turned sideways to indicate a man standing about twenty feet away, watching.

The tall one with big hands. Two wings of bronze flashed on his helmet, showing him to be of a higher rank than a mere Solit; Centenor Jakhron, of course, to whom Arcmas had been introduced yesterday. Arcmas hesitated, but Hanthor, who was already walking away, turned back to him impatiently.

"Well, soldier?" he snapped. He turned on his heel and kept going, in his short, quick stride. Arcmas had no choice but to follow, so he did, with a slight shrug for his friends. Left behind, Hennelyn and Nik watched the meeting between them. Arcmas saluted smartly, and then he and the two men strolled away together.

"You see?" Hennelyn whispered to Nik. "It's starting already. They'll keep him busy now the whole of the time left, I'm sure of it. But I'm going to make sure that I get a last goodbye, in spite of them all!" Nik gave her a look of admiration.

"How are you going to do it?" he inquired. Hennelyn told him. "And you can come too, if you want!"

But Nik's eyes dropped away from her excited face. Uncomfortably he told her, "But Henna, you - you know that I can't. It's all right for you; you're General Kanow's daughter. But I'm only a servant. A thing like that, if I did it… "

Hennelyn was immediately sympathetic.

"No, that's alright, Nik. I shouldn't have suggested it. I forget sometimes - well, you've never been only a servant to Arcmas and me, you know."

"I know," he told her. "Your plan's a good one. I'm sure it will really annoy the ambassador!" They both laughed.

# Chapter Five

It soon looked as though Hennelyn's prediction was coming true. General Kanow did eventually finish his report for Tol Lorsumn, but by then Arcmas had been swallowed up into the ranks of the ambassador's men and was not to be seen. When it was time to leave, there had been no opportunity for Tai and Arcmas to talk together at all. The best Tai could do was to come outside the gate and stand there watching for Arcmas to pass by, with several members of his staff who had been close to the boy. Echthus and Lisha were there, with Jaero Lite and even the little maid Dewdra, scanning the crowd for a last glimpse.

Nik peered out round the huge gate support pole, away from the others, while the ambassador's escort filed by on their horses, saluting. They went in rows of five abreast, led by Marshal Stokhor.

It was hard to pick out Arcmas, though, as row on row of identical uniforms passed. Tai was also craning his neck to see someone else he was missing. His daughter. He had no idea where she had gone.

Wait! Was that Steed, the big black gelding in the middle? It seemed so, and then Tai saw the telltale wings on the rider, flowing down on either side of the horse. Arcmas saluted just like all the others as they passed the general. Just as he was about to go by, his arm came up and he released something into the air. A hawk, which flew up high and emitted a screeching cry.

It swooped down at Tai and revealed itself to be Glider, Arcmas's special pet. Tai raised his arm and Glider landed on it, pinching him with its talons through his sleeve as it settled on him. Arcmas had found a way to say goodbye after all, sending his hawk to single Tai out. Glider fixed the man with his beady eye, giving voice to several squeaks and croons in hawk fashion. Then it fluttered back up into the air, and Tai saw Arcmas give a small wave as he left home and family behind.

Tai swallowed hard, aware of Siras Thraulor's searching eyes as he looked on from his mount right next to the general. Siras's face had had a smug expression on it all this time - at least as much as his rigid features would allow.

In his smooth, cultured voice he addressed Tai, "Well, General

Kanow, I do thank you for a pleasant stay - again. You have always been a loyal soldier, and I don't doubt that the emperor will be pleased to hear how you have cared for this special recruit all these years. He may even wish to reward you. After my report, of course."

Tai knew the right response.

"Thank you, Your Excellency, you are too kind."

"Yes. Well, we must be off. Farewell until next time, General. Come, Hanthor."

He touched up his horse and rode off with Hanthor close behind, as Tai and his household either saluted or bowed him on.

For a few minutes the remaining ranks of the soldiers passed by, and then the entire convoy began to move off among the fields and ravines, quickly shrinking to insignificance under the endless pearly heavens. Finally, the household of the Outpost seemed to heave a collective sigh and slowly walk back to the house.

Suddenly, a rider came at full tilt through the gate, scattering people before her. This, at least, solved the mystery of Tai's missing daughter, for it was Hennelyn, leaning low over the neck of her golden horse with her fox-fur coat's large sleeves billowing out behind her. The startled folk followed her with their eyes. But Tai waved a dismissive hand; there wasn't any way of stopping her now, whatever it was that she had in mind. He followed everyone back into the grounds of the Outpost and strode towards the stables.


Arcmas rode on in the midst of the crowd of soldiers. The sounds of cold creaking leather and thudding hooves surrounded him in all directions. His new trainer, Centenor Jakhron, rode a big grey to his left, but other than this man whom he knew very slightly, Arcmas was surrounded by strangers. He stared ahead of himself moodily, not giving in to the urge to look back.

He had spent his last hours at home surrounded by these men; he had eaten with them, been stared at by them, been introduced around, and had listened to endless briefings until now he felt little more than numb inside, except for a cold grey lump which seemed to sit low in his guts. He had not even said a proper good-bye to his father, except for the half-baked stunt with Glider.

*But what can I do about it now? All I can do,* he reasoned to himself, *is to be the best soldier I can, to make sure that any reports about me that reach General Kanow will be good ones.*

As he was gloomily occupied with these thoughts, he suddenly heard a commotion somewhere far back in the ranks. The men around him were craning their necks trying to see what was wrong but were too disciplined to talk. So Arcmas looked, too. He noticed that there was a single rider that had completely broken ranks and was meandering through the neat rows of horses, throwing them into disarray until they closed up ranks behind the disturbance. As this rider drew closer, Arcmas got one clear glimpse through the sea of helmeted heads. He gasped, and involuntarily reined Steed in to a stop. The horses and riders behind him followed suit in confusion.

"Hennelyn!" he called to her in wonder.

She heard and turned her tousled blonde head in his direction. Her golden hair and red fur jacket were bright splashes of color against the monotone background of dark grey helms and brown uniforms. With a sunny smile, she spurred up through the rows and reined Wingfoot over beside Steed, forcing a place between Arcmas and Jakhron, causing many a bemused look from the men around her. Someone barked an order, and the ranks at the back moved forward again, Hennelyn among them.

"Arcmas!" she panted. "Hello, big brother!"

Arcmas frowned at her in astonishment, but could not hold in a smile, even though it arrived with a severe shake of his head.

"Henna, what are you doing here?"

"Don't you remember your wish? When you said you wished Father or I could come along? Well, here I am!" At his look she added, "Yes, I know it's not for long. But I couldn't let Ambassador Thraulor have it all his own way, could I?"

"Henna," Arcmas warned quietly. "What do you mean?"

She also lowered her voice. "You *know* what I mean... the ambassador, and I guess the emperor, too, don't want you to remember that we're a family anymore. But you won't forget... will you?"

He responded softly, "Could I forget my own sister?"

"And your own father? What about him?" she prodded. When Arcmas didn't answer, she continued, "It wasn't his fault, you know. He would have spent every last moment with you if he could have, I'm sure of it. But he's always the obedient soldier. He had his orders."

There was a pause, and then Arcmas added sadly, "There... there was something that I wanted to tell him."

"Well, I'll tell him for you, if you like," she assured him.

He grinned sidewise at her. "You're really something, do you know that?"

"Oh, I know," she giggled. "It took me a little while to get up the nerve to follow the regiment. I just didn't want you to start off completely alone."

They laughed quietly. Just then, into the middle of this nice visit rode trouble in the form of Siras Thraulor - with Hanthor not far behind. Jakhron and the man next to him moved their horses out of the ranks so that the ambassador could ride in and come up next to Hennelyn. Arcmas and the soldiers around him all saluted Siras's arrival. But the ambassador only had eyes for Hennelyn.

"Hello again, young mistress!" he greeted her dryly.

She turned her windblown head towards him and inclined it in respect. Her clear eyes regarded him steadily. The cold had pinched her cheeks into high color and polished the blue of her sparkling eyes, her unconscious beauty drawing many looks from the soldiers.

"Good day, Ambassador," she replied graciously.

"Does your father know where you are at this moment?"

She answered with aplomb, "He saw me leave, Your Excellency. But he doesn't know what I am doing. This was all my idea."

"I see. And just what, precisely, are you doing?"

"Well, sir, I just wanted to be with my brother a little bit longer. I didn't want him to be all alone on the road right from the start."

Siras's eyelids fell halfway over his cold grey eyes, making them look sinister.

"Young lady, I know you are only a civilian. But I suspect that even you understand that you are to present yourself to the officer in charge of any squadron, before approaching anyone else. And you also know what it means to 'break ranks without leave,' don't you?"

"Yes of course, Your Excellency, but-"

"Well, then, Mistress Kanow, you see before you the highest-ranking commanding officer of this company. If you want to speak to one of my soldiers, you must go through me. Now, follow me, if you please." When she cast an uncertain glance at Arcmas and hesitated, Siras added in a low, falsely friendly tone which made her skin crawl, "I can assure you, Miss Hennelyn, your 'brother' is not alone. He is ours now. Come with me."

He reined his horse out of the ranks, and Hennelyn reluctantly followed. When they were stopped outside of the moving rows of mounted men, Siras turned his horse's head towards her and said condescendingly, "If you need an escort to help you find your way home, I shall be most pleased to provide one. Hanthor, call out a man…"

"Oh no, Your Excellency, that won't be necessary, I know the way," Hennelyn interrupted him - something that few ever dared - "but if you'll excuse me, sir, I'll just say my last goodbye to Arcmas!" Her own audacity made her head spin. Before Siras could react, she touched up her horse with her heels and burst into the ranks of men again.

She came up beside her brother once more, breathless and flushed. But behind her she could hear the shouted orders, and the whole company came to a sudden halt, horses tossing their heads and dancing in place.

Into the relative quiet that followed, she panted, "Now, Arcmas, you had a last message for Father, I think? Tell me what it is quick, because His High-and-Mightiness is trying to send me off home."

Arcmas only said, "Henna, you'd better get away. You know Siras is trouble."

"Oh, never mind that! What was it that you wanted to tell Father, and didn't get the chance to?"

He dropped his eyes. When he glanced over his shoulder, he could see two soldiers approaching his position. Their hands rested on their scabbards. It was now or never.

He swallowed and stammered, "It was just that I … I never really told him, and I wanted Father to know that I …" but he couldn't get it out.

"That you love him?" Hennelyn supplied quietly. He nodded slightly, not daring to look her in the eye. She reached out her hand, and he grasped it in his.

"Okay, Arcmas. I'll tell Father." Her eyes misted slightly. "Goodbye…"

"Goodbye, Hennelyn." They did as much of the secret handshake they could from the backs of horses. Then, just as the two soldiers drew up next to Hennelyn, swords out, she urged Wingfoot away through the ranks and galloped off.

The two soldiers watched her leave. Then they sheathed their swords and turned around, back to their assigned positions. Before long, the column of soldiers was on the move again, responding to a marching order.

Arcmas found that he was grinning just a little bit until Siras Thraulor rode up outside his row and stayed there a long minute, fixing his colorless eyes on Arcmas with a look that was shrewdly calculating. Under his stare, the warm feeling drained away, and Arcmas wondered if Hennelyn's stunt might affect his future with this company of men, and if it did, how. Then the ambassador dug in his heels and galloped away towards his place at the head of the line, the inevitable Hanthor trailing behind him.

Hennelyn held Wingfoot at a gallop for a while, letting him enjoy himself. The sun was behind a thin cloud cover, washing everything in softly veiled gold. The air had a cool taste of fall, and it lifted Hennelyn's spirits. For once she felt she had triumphed over Siras Thraulor. Wingfoot tired and slowed into an easy trot for home, needing no guidance from her.

Shortly, another rider appeared out of a gully on the rolling plain in front of her. It didn't take her long to identify him as her father, on his tall bay stallion. The horse, as always, was recognizable by the way he swung his big hooves out sideways as he loped along. Father and daughter came face to face, reining in to a stop. They looked at each other's wild hair and flaming cheeks and grinned. Tai spoke first.

"Well, daughter?" he asked, in a sort of invitation.

"I rode with Arcmas for a little bit."

Tai nodded seriously. "And how did he seem?"

"He looked a little lost in the crowd. Too young, and his uniform is too big." She saw that her father's head bowed a bit lower, so she added quickly, "He sent a message, though. Something he wanted me to tell you."

Tai raised his head again and searched her face.

"He said... he loved you, Father."

Tai gazed at the horizon beyond her. In a dry tone he asked, "Did the ambassador give you any trouble?"

"Not really. For once."

Tai gave a short laugh. "That would be a first." He wheeled his horse around and continued, "Come on, my girl. Let's go home." So they started off, side by side, now a smaller family of two.

After Arcmas left, fall arrived, in all its warm palette of auburns and saffrons. It was brief and quickly followed by winter. Day by day, warm spells followed by snowfall, the coldest season spread its white cloak and icy breath. The soldiers were kept busy cutting wood for their own fires as well as those of the general's household. Farm families did the same. Out came the fruit and vegetable preserves from the farm homes, laid up both for them and their regiment of soldiers. Everyone went about in fur-lined cloaks and boots.

For Hennelyn and Nik, it seemed as if they had each lost a right arm. They hardly knew what to do with themselves now that one of their number was missing. They didn't seem up to their usual mischief. As the winter deepened, Hennelyn still caught herself watching for Arcmas to come in at the schoolroom door, or when she was at her archery, looking up into his tree where he always used to perch. The shock of his absence did not seem to diminish.

As for General Tai Kanow, if he missed his young son, it was not apparent in his manner. He had received new orders, and now the regiment of the outpost was busy felling trees and preparing a new building site east of the present town. First up would be another huge spruce fence inside which buildings would be erected. The area being cleared was three times as large as the first Starkhon settlement and would probably take a long time to complete. It appeared that Emperor Tol Lorsumn expected to settle more Starkhons here eventually.

More and more, the bunjis were in everyone's minds. No one spoke of them, but everyone was thinking about them, especially when it got to be the middle of December. If things went as they had last winter, there were only two weeks left before the bunjis held their winter festival, very close to the Outpost.

One day as Tai and Hennelyn watched the soldiers work on the new site, she asked, "Father, do you think the bunjis will really light their special fires again?"

"I don't know, Hennelyn," Tai said in answer to her question. "I suppose we will just have to wait and see. Of course, if they do, we're hoping to catch one of them. Last year we were taken by surprise. This year we will be ready."

She sighed, not noticing her father's questioning glance.

"Well, they might have their festival, but I don't really feel like celebrating Longest Night if Arcmas won't be here. Who's going to drape the streamers in the hall?" she wondered.

Tai shrugged.

"I suppose we'll have to use a ladder this year."

To Hennelyn he seemed not to care at all about the Starkhon solstice holiday. She deduced that he was distracted by the hope of a bunji capture, since their midwinter celebration took place eight days before the Starkhons' celebration.

"I hope we get a letter from Arcmas when the Longest Night supplies arrive. Father... do you suppose they'll let him come home and visit?"

Tai roused himself out of a sort of reverie to reply, "I don't know. Perhaps when the new squadron of men arrives in the summer, Arcmas will come with them. Yes... and I'll be receiving a replacement marshal, too. It doesn't seem like Marshal Maraton has been here six months already."

After this vague sentence, Hennelyn's father walked away from her into the work site to direct a group of soldiers who weren't doing just as he wanted. *So much for talking about Arcmas, she thought.*

Two weeks passed quickly. The night of the bunji festival arrived. Hennelyn and Nik dressed warmly, got supplies together, and climbed the wooden ladder up into the west corner tower to wait until nightfall. It was cold up there, but it was also the perfect vantage point for them to observe the bunji rites. The children remembered from the year before that the fire performance was dazzling, though they had only caught the tail end of it last time.

First of all, the two youngsters built a small fire in the grate (wood kindly provided by the staff) and began to set the scene. On the tipsy wooden table they piled their blankets, cups, spoons, a kettle of water for making 'hot hop,' a child's treat made from roasted barley, milk, and sugar. Flints and other fire-making tools were always present in the towers. For seats, they used a couple of rough-hewn log benches.

Hennelyn and Nik hung the water in a kettle over the fire to boil and dragged one of the benches over to the window to stand on. In this way, they could comfortably rest their elbows on the thick stone window ledge and look out. They were not exactly sure where to look, but the fire show last year had been somewhere to the north of the Outpost. Luckily, the sky was clear, and the rotund moon was slowly plodding to its zenith. The stars sparkled above like a broken and scattered necklace of white gems. The voices of coyotes wailed eerily, like a choir of wandering souls.

Nothing happened before the water came to a boil, and the children snuggled up in a shared blanket with their hands warming on their hot cups. They whispered to one another, their breath smoking in the cold air. Then, something happened at last.

First there came the low but rising sound of music, carried towards them on the frigid breeze, voices and simple instruments together. Hennelyn's hair prickled at the back of her neck, and she wondered how many hundreds of bunjis it took, out there, to produce that sound. She remembered that last winter this singing had been bolder and started earlier in the evening. Now it seemed that the bunjis were more cautious than before.

The beautiful and unmistakably joyful singing suddenly ended, and then came what the children were waiting for. The bunjis began to light long snakes of flammable fuel that had been carefully arranged on the ground - some of it draped even over the frozen branches of the trees.

No Starkhon knew how it was done, but the fire caught quickly along these piles, and burned just long enough so that watchers like Hennelyn and Nik could see pictures outlined in the running lines of flame, pictures that grew more elaborate and beautiful as they spread. There were the forms of animals, trees, and bunji figures, and at crucial points in the fiery scene, a bright flame shot out momentarily as though to indicate action. These bursts could be any color of the rainbow: hot red, sparkling white, vivid green, or neon blue like the flames nearest a burning log.

For a few seconds one scene was gloriously complete, and then the fiery outlines winked out, and another conflagration began in a different place. The sight thrilled Hennelyn and Nik as they looked on from their excellent vantage point. The fiery drawings raced up and down but never seemed to get out of control.

The last scenario, like the year before, contained one huge figure that was probably a bunji but might have been Starkhon for all Hennelyn could tell, who twinkled into being from the feet up. When his head was reached, a bright white ring sizzled into existence around it, shooting sparks and dazzling the eye. With him the fire-story ended, leaving Hennelyn breathless and strangely moved. She longed to know what the story depicted and especially who that last man was. *But why do the bunjis repeat this performance with danger so near at hand?* she wondered. *What's the purpose of it all? They themselves cannot possibly see it from their viewpoint on the ground.*

When all had gone dark, Nik yawned hugely and wanted to go to his warm bed. Hennelyn missed Arcmas a lot at that moment. She remembered the long talk they'd had last year about what they'd seen.

She climbed down with Nik and walked back to the house, leaving the makings of their drinks behind to be retrieved the next day. They said goodnight to each other before parting. In her bed with the furry covers pulled up to her chin, Hennelyn did not go to sleep at once. Instead, she replayed what she had seen in her mind's eye and pondered it. Homesickness for Arcmas and the awe of the bunji fire-story seemed to stir all together in her mind and heart, and later that night she had a strange dream.

She dreamed that she was somehow floating alongside Arcmas as he drifted between the flickering bunji fires below and the moonlight above. His light hawk's eyes studied the ground intensely, reflecting the firelight. Then he suddenly swooped down low, returning soon after to Hennelyn's side. She saw that now he clutched a small, round-bellied bunji to his chest. Although she had never seen one in waking life, the bunji's face was clearly detailed. Its complexion was dark and muddy with fear as it shivered and watched the earth rush past beneath.

Then, just as Hennelyn started to ache with pity for the creature, a blinding light burst down upon all three of them. She saw that Arcmas had come to confusion in mid-air; he had dropped his quarry and was trying to block the light with his arms held up before his face. Then as Hennelyn watched, half-blinded herself, she saw with terror that it was Arcmas who was dropping helplessly to earth, while the bunji, smiling in radiant joy, continued to rise higher and higher until he was swallowed up into the brilliance.

### Letter from Arcmas - October:

*Hi Hennelyn. I don't know how to write letters — never tried before! But I see that the other recruits write to their families, so I thought I'd try. Father isn't really the letter-reading type, so I wrote to you instead. It's a good use of this journal that I got on my birthday, too. It took two whole weeks to ride all the way to Khuntz. Glider followed me part of the way, but I sent him back. I didn't want him to leave his home, even if I had to. All of the other soldiers stayed in Khuntz. But after five days, the ambassador, Centenor Jakhron, Marshall Stokhor, and that little weasel Hanthor and I left for Glott, the next biggest city, bigger than Khuntz. The new recruits from the Outpost came, too. You know them; Marshall Maraton's son and that Donotar Stankhreed (perfect name for him!). They were two of the boys who threw me down the well. That trip took another week.*

*I have never been so sick of riding or saddling and unsaddling Steed! Three weeks of riding ten hours a day. It felt like I had never been anywhere or done anything else. There are a couple of small villages between Khuntz and Glott. In Glott, some buildings are made of stone and have real glass windows, like our home in Flaethe. So many more Starkhons than we've ever seen before!*

*I miss you more than I thought I would. All of you. If you are wondering, I haven't made any friends yet. I am younger than all of the other solits, and of course*

*I am different. People are always staring, especially when all of us men undress for the night in the barracks. It's very embarrassing to do that in front of everyone.*

*Ambassador Siras Thraulor has told me that we aren't going all the way to Starkha yet.*

*I keep the crest you made me and Nik's wooden horse on me all the time, even when I am sleeping. Father's cuilla, too. Well, goodbye for now. I will write again soon.*

# Chapter Six

When Hennelyn awoke the next morning, she didn't remember her dream. She jumped out of bed before Dewdra the maid was even awake and dressed herself to go downstairs.

As she sat down to breakfast a little later, she noticed a strange silence among the two Luinians and her father at the table. As her porridge was spooned into a bowl by a servant, she glanced around at the others, frowning. Jaero Lite would not look at her, and Lisha seemed upset. Only the general appeared to be in good humor.

"Eat up, my girl," Tai urged, "we have a busy day ahead of us!"

"What's happened?" Hennelyn asked suspiciously. Her father mopped at his mouth before answering, revealing a smug smile that the napkin had seemed to plant there.

"My soldiers brought me something last night after the bunji fires had gone out. Would you like to see him?"

Hennelyn was confused. "Him? Who... what do you mean?" Then, with sudden realization and alarm, "Oh! Do you mean to say you've got - you didn't manage to catch - or did you?"

"Yes," confirmed her father. "We've caught a bunji prisoner. We had soldiers out on horseback during their festival, trying to find them as they lit their fires. It was difficult. There were literally miles of fuel lines laid out. But one of them got caught by his clothing on something. Solit Collaton happened to be nearby and captured him before he escaped. He's a young one. These little people have some spirit. Collaton said that the creature was as slippery as a fish, and bit him on the hand - twice!"

Without thinking, Hennelyn blurted out in dismay, "Oh no, Father!" Tai stared at her. She blushed but said nothing more.

He continued, matter-of-factly, "We're holding him in the east tower."

"For interrogation?" Hennelyn guessed. She could not seem to slow her heart, wondering if anyone could hear how it was thudding away. She had been hoping more than she realized that their search for bunjis would turn out to be fruitless once more.

"Yes. For interrogation. Hennelyn, I think it's about time that you were schooled in military dealings. After breakfast I want you to come with me and see the prisoner."

Hennelyn looked up and met his eyes.

"Alright, Father," she agreed, pleased to hear that her voice did not waver.

"Eat up, then - I'll wait for you. And Lisha," he continued sternly as the governess stirred uneasily beside Hennelyn, "if I want your opinion, I will ask for it."

"Yes sir," assented the Luinian woman, "but I do think that if Raethena were here-"

"Raethena is not here," the general broke in sternly, "and I will do as I see fit." His voice made the hall ring even though he had not raised it.

"Yes sir," said Lisha quickly. In a more temperate tone, Tai added, "After all, she is almost fifteen and will not be needing a governess very much longer. I am sure she will still value your advice though, for you are much more than a servant here, you know that, Lisha. Hennelyn, do you need more time to finish eating?"

She looked at her half-full bowl of cooling porridge with a fading appetite.

"I'm... full. We may as well go to the tower now."

"Very well. Jaero Lite, I don't think we will need you today."

"What? You took Jaero Lite there already?" Hennelyn asked. Tai nodded. "Of course. As soon as the prisoner was brought in."

"Your father thought that my knowledge of coastal bunji speech would be a help. But I am afraid it wasn't. The dialects are very different," the tutor explained. Tai rose from his chair, and Hennelyn followed suit.

"Very good then. Let's go, my girl. We will all meet again over lunch," Tai said as he turned and led Hennelyn from the hall. She followed with her head high and her step as sure as she could make it. Nik entered just then with more firewood and heard what the two Luinians said to one another as soon as Tai and Hennelyn had left.

At first Lisha looked as though she had much to say about the proceedings, but Jaero Lite mumbled, "They are Starkhons. They will act as Starkhons act. We cannot change that."

"Up to now I have raised her to be as genteel as I could," Lisha disagreed doggedly. "Just as her mother Raethena would have wanted. She wouldn't have allowed her daughter to be... be militarized like she has been these last seven years... to become just like all the rest of them…" Her lips snapped shut and trembled indignantly. Jaero Lite was silent for a moment.

"Don't sell yourself short, Lisha," he mused. "Or Hennelyn either. She may still surprise us." He nodded prophetically at his companion. Nik put more wood on the blaze and tried to look as though he wasn't eavesdropping.

Tai and Hennelyn arrived together at the east tower, Hennelyn a step behind her father. They knocked and entered it to find two soldiers guarding it at ground level. This tower was different from the west one. While the west tower had permanent stairs built to reach the upper level, the east one only had a ladder which could be easily set up or down. The trap door above them was quite high and could be bolted shut from the outside, like it was now.

The guards saluted their general smartly.

"Decenor Collaton, do you have anything to report? Has the prisoner told you anything?" Tai demanded of the stockier man.

"Not very much, sir. He seems not to know much of the Common Tongue."

"Really? I thought they all knew it well."

"Apparently not these bunjis out here, sir."

"Let's go up and have a look at him. Lead the way, Decenor."

"Yes, sir."

Collaton turned to climb the ladder and opened the trap door. When he had disappeared through it, Tai followed. Hennelyn brought up the rear. The remaining guard stayed where he was.

As they climbed into the upper room, another solit saluted them. He had been lounging against the stone-block wall next to the single window in the room, but now he stood stiffly to attention. There was little else in the room. A bucket stood near the fireplace, and some bundles of wood were stacked there, too. There was a tray containing a bowl of untouched porridge on the hearth; it reminded Hennelyn of her own unfinished breakfast. The only other object was a rough-hewn wooden chair, sitting facing the window. Huddled into this was the captured bunji. The small creature did not look around as they entered but continued staring up at the patch of sky visible through the high unshuttered square window.

"At ease, Solit," Tai told this other soldier, and the man let his saluting arm drop. "Has our prisoner given you any trouble?" The man's face creased into a one-sided smile.

"He's no trouble at all, sir," he reported. Tai nodded. He

approached the chair, and motioned to Hennelyn to do the same.

"Here he is, child," he told her. "What do you think of him?" She came slowly closer. This was her first real look at their kind.

The bunji's complexion was darker than a Starkhon's, his eyes a very dark brown or perhaps black. They were slightly glazed at the moment. There was a reddish bruise on his left cheekbone, or where the bone would be if his face were not so round. His tousled hair was black and cut short, with straight bangs lying on his forehead. He had on breeches of white rabbit fur, and his shirt appeared to be made of some rough tan wool, with a drawstring closure at the neck. One of the sleeves was rolled up.

On the floor beside him lay a thick hooded tunic of white fur, and his boots were of the same material. Hennelyn wondered how Decenor Collaton had even been able to see him against the snow at night. If the bunji stood up, Hennelyn estimated that he would have reached just under her shoulder in height. He was not a child but still young, for his cheeks were smooth and hairless.

As father and daughter stood in front of him, blocking his view of the window, his eyes came into slow focus on General Kanow. They widened in fear, and he seemed to shrink further back into the unyielding chair. But then he switched his gaze to Hennelyn. The Starkhons were unprepared for his reaction.

Astonishment dawned on his face, and his mouth opened to make an almost perfect O. He spoke some words in his own language, and then two in the Common Tongue with a strong accent - but very clearly: "...sun child..." he said in wonder. Then he thrust himself out of the chair and approached Hennelyn on unsteady legs. Tai and the decenor exchanged significant glances, and they backed away from Hennelyn.

As they did, the bunji came ever closer until he looked up into Hennelyn's face. What he saw there must have reassured him, for he said again, "Sunchild. You... sunchild."

She didn't answer, not understanding his loopy walk or his dull gaze.

"What's wrong with him?" she questioned the soldier over her shoulder. The man glanced at Tai for permission to answer.

"Just a little serum to relax him, maybe make him talk, Mistress Hennelyn. Your father's orders," he told her. "But he's said more to you in the Common Tongue just now than we've heard yet." And the bunji spoke again, with difficulty.

"You... here. Is...in here, locked in. Like me?"

Hennelyn paused for a moment, considering, then answered, "No, I am not a prisoner. I live here. These are my people," she told him, with a sweeping gesture to include the others. The bunji seemed bewildered. Then, to everyone's surprise, he went down on his knees before her, hands upturned.

"You help. Get out. You help. Please," he begged, his dark face tilted up to hers. Hennelyn looked over at Tai helplessly, who seemed pleased at this turn of events.

"Well, we never expected this," he remarked. "He must realize that you are one-half Luinian; we know that they have traded with the coastal bunjis before. My girl, I think you are about to become our best interrogator. What if we left you alone with him for a little while? You could talk to him, find out what he knows."

"But Father! I don't know what information you want."

"Anything you can get him to say may be useful. Just try to draw him out. Solit, put him back in the chair." The soldier strode up and started to drag the bunji away.

"No!" the captive cried out. He reached for Hennelyn. "Help me! Help!" But it was no use. The Starkhon with his superior strength forced the small creature back into the chair, where he froze with his arms up defensively, panting and piercing Hennelyn with a desperate gaze. Hennelyn turned away abruptly and moved quickly to the trapdoor, starting down the ladder. She boiled with indignation over the prisoner's treatment, and she could feel tears of sympathy pricking at the backs of her eyes. But she wasn't going to let these soldiers or her father have the satisfaction of seeing how upset she was. When she reached the bottom of the ladder, she marched quickly through the door of the prison tower. But her father's voice stopped her just outside it.

"Hennelyn, wait!"

She dashed an errant tear away before he could see. Before he could speak, she blurted, "I'll do it!"

"What?" Tai looked closely into her face.

"I'll do as you asked, Father. I'll talk to him." She gazed at him steadily.

He nodded after a moment, satisfied. "All right, my girl. Tomorrow we start."

The next morning Hennelyn managed to choke down some breakfast in her room. She didn't want to see the expressions on the Luinians' faces, though she knew they wouldn't dare say anything. It was

56

foolish to worry about the opinions of servants, but – she couldn't help it.

After she had finished eating, Hennelyn walked purposefully out to the east tower. She hesitated outside the door for a moment. Then she lifted her chin and loudly knocked on it.

The guard that had been there yesterday cracked open the door to see who it was, and then opened it wide for her. He inclined his head as she stepped in.

"You are early, Mistress. Neither the general nor Solit Nakhanor have been here yet." Hennelyn nodded. She glanced up at the trapdoor and the soldier followed suit.

"The bunji has tried to escape a couple of times," he offered.

"When did he do that? And how?"

"In the middle of the night. He was just testing the door to see if it was locked. The solits on duty were pretending to sleep to see what he would do. They caught him as soon as he reached the bottom of the ladder, of course."

He smiled, apparently at the cleverness of his fellows, but Hennelyn did not appreciate the joke. She moved to the ladder and put her hand on it.

"Is the bunji awake?" she asked.

"Yes, miss, and the guard, too. We've already passed their breakfast up to them. Would you like me to go up first and open the trapdoor for you, Mistress Hennelyn?" offered the soldier.

"No, thank you, Solit. I'll do it."

She climbed up and fumbled with the catch over her head for some moments before she got it undone. Then she pushed the sturdy door open. It was very heavy and cost her quite a bit of effort before she managed to bang it down to level. The soldier below her went back to the breakfast she had interrupted.

Hennelyn climbed into the tower, looking around as she did. The bunji sat by the wall opposite the window, leaning against the wall, his head resting on his arms so that she could not see his face. The other guard, a different one from yesterday, was sitting in the chair eating the last of his breakfast from his tray. Another tray holding a bowl sat on the hearth of the fireplace, where the fire had burned low. The room was downright chilly. The man stood in respect when he saw who had entered, the cup in his hand sending up a steam in the cool air. The bunji did not move.

"Good morning, young mistress. Your father told me to expect you sometime today, when I took up my post last night. I didn't think you would be the first person I saw, though. I thought it was the next man coming to spell me off." Hennelyn spent this explanation studying the bunji in the shadows.

"Is he all right?" she wanted to know.

"As right as rain, miss, though he did give me some trouble in the night; I suppose you've heard."

"Yes, the other Solit told me." At the sound of her voice, the bunji stirred, standing up. As he stepped away from the wall, Hennelyn heard the drag of a chain. She quickly approached the captive. She saw that he had been fastened to one of the iron rings in the wall by a manacle around one ankle and a short length of chain.

"What is this?" she demanded with an edge to her voice. The soldier shrugged.

"I got tired of wrestling him away from the trap door."

"Take it off!"

"But Miss- "

"Now!" she commanded in a fair imitation of her father.

"Alright, Mistress Hennelyn," the soldier said, giving in. He took a key from his belt and knelt down to remove the iron anklet. As he threw it aside and stood, the bunji backed away from him into the abutment of the fireplace. Hennelyn stepped between them.

"You are dismissed, Solit," she told him firmly.

"What?"

"I said, you can go."

"I would if I could, mistress, but it's against orders. I can't leave until my replacement arrives. We have to report all activities that take place here."

"Then stand further away - over there!" Hennelyn pointed. The soldier eyed her grimly, but he went. He stopped against the wall at the furthest point away, which was maybe fifteen feet in all. It was not a large place.

Hennelyn looked into the bunji's face. He regarded her calmly in return, some of the fear fading from his eyes. But she could see the signs of a sleepless night. Still, at least he was no longer drugged, for his eyes were bright and clear. She wondered if he remembered much of the day before. "Are you all right?" she asked softly, switching to the common speech. He gave no answer, but she could see him relax just a little. "Let me look at that ankle."

She took his arm gently and guided him to the hearth to sit

58

down. He no longer had his fur boots on, just thin foot covers of soft buckskin leather. Hennelyn pushed up his breeches a bit to examine the skin which had been circled by the iron band. It looked a bit chafed and red but didn't seem to be sore.

"Do you remember me?" Hennelyn pressed him. "You saw me yesterday."

He hesitated, then gave the slightest of nods.

"Sun child," he whispered.

"Yes!" She smiled, nodding. From behind her came the soldier's sardonic voice.

"Since he likes you so much, see if you can get him to eat, Mistress Hennelyn. I can't. I've heard he hasn't eaten a bite since he got here. Drinks water only."

She looked at the tray on the hearth near them, and grimaced at the mass of cold congealing porridge in the bowl.

"He won't eat this stuff now, that's for sure. Send the solit down below for something good from the kitchens. Some berry preserves and fresh bread. And maybe a bit of deer jerky. If I'm brought that, I'll see what I can do."

The soldier moved to the open trapdoor and called down to the other man, telling him what Hennelyn wanted.

She tried to talk to the bunji, to draw him out, but although he studied her face intently, he would not reply. A gleam of suspicion in his dark eyes had replaced the eager gaze of yesterday. And no wonder. He had seen the blonde slip of a girl give orders to a grown man, and more than that, she was obeyed. He must be wondering how she fit into this strange society that had imprisoned him.

The change of the guard and the food that Hennelyn had requested arrived together. A new guard poked his head up through the trap door, and when he had climbed up, Hennelyn saw the loaded basket he'd brought along. He greeted Hennelyn and brought the food over. It was covered with a cloth, but Hennelyn recognized the irresistible scent of fresh bread wafting from it.

"Thank you, Solit," said Hennelyn. "I know you can't leave us alone here, but do you think you could take that chair and sit over on the other side there? Try not to watch us."

"Well, mistress, my orders are-"

"Come on, Solit, you don't think that the prisoner is a match for me?"

The soldier regarded the young bunji's slight form and grinned.

"No, Mistress Hennelyn. I wager you're right." With a wink, he left to do as she had said, dragging the heavy chair to the far wall with ease. It creaked as he sat in it, and then he fumbled through his tunic pockets, rolling out a smoke with what he'd found. Hennelyn turned back to the bunji youth and pulled the cloth from the basket. She saw that there were four slices of warm bread, berry jam, and jerky inside, just as she had ordered. There was also a small leather flask of something to drink.

"Here you are. It's for you. Eat!"

She elaborately motioned eating. He understood her all right, but he stood up abruptly and turned his back on her. Not quickly enough, though, to hide his longing for the food. Hennelyn thought for a moment. Then she took a small piece of jerky out and started to eat it herself. The crisped edges made a satisfying crunch in her teeth.

"Mmmm," she breathed, smacking her lips. She tore another bite off with her teeth, watching the bunji's short back. Finally, he turned slowly around, and sat down again beside the basket, his eyes fixed on the contents. Hennelyn picked up a slice of bread and spread jam on it with the provided spoon as he watched. Then she grabbed his hand, and placed the bread in it. His resistance crumbled and he ate it in five bites, with obvious relish. Then he turned his attention to the remaining food.

With the jerky, he decided to include a drink from the flask. He took a large swallow, immediately coughing afterward.

"What?" Hennelyn asked with a smile. He offered her the flask and she sloshed some into her mouth. Then she understood. It had been filled with strong Starkhon ale. She was used to it, and downed it with ease. Impressed, the bunji reached eagerly for the flask again. He did not choke over his second drink of it. He burped instead. She saw with satisfaction that he had eaten every crumb of food and obviously felt better for it.

The bunji leaned back against the stonework of the fireplace, closing weary eyes. But then they snapped open again and focused sharply on Hennelyn. Calculating.

"You... you are good," he observed. "Not-" His eyes flicked grimly towards the soldier with unmistakable ire. The man in question was merely relaxing and blowing smoke towards the ceiling, but Hennelyn realized that he was thinking of his rough treatment when he carefully touched his bruised face.

He went on: "...but you stay here. Not prisoner?"

Hennelyn nodded.

"I live here, yes. I'm not a prisoner."

"Who - who are you?" the bunji wanted to know. Hennelyn did not know how to reply. It depended on what exactly he meant. He most likely wanted to know how much authority she had, or how she could possibly have any at all.

After a moment she answered simply, with careful enunciation, "Hennelyn. My name is Hennelyn." She gestured at herself.

"Hen-lin," he repeated uncertainly.

"Hen-ne-lyn. Yes. Who are you?"

She waited to hear his name, but he did not offer it.

Hennelyn stayed in the tower all morning. Though the bunji was willing enough to stumble along in the trade speech, they really didn't get past the basics. She found herself answering more questions than she asked. At length she gave up. But as she stood to leave, he caught her by the edge of her tunic and held on.

"You... come back?" he asked nervously. She smiled at him.

"Yes, I'll come back. Don't worry. No one is going to hurt you today, if you are quiet." He nodded and let go. The soldier saluted her as she approached the trap door.

"Goodbye, miss."

She paused and stared hard at the man, heavy-muscled and coarse-featured. He looked familiar but she'd forgotten his name. He was just one of the hundred living here.

"You heard what I promised him, didn't you?"

"Yes, miss."

"Don't make a liar out of me, Solit."

"No, young mistress."

She had to be satisfied with that, even though she saw that his eyes glinted with amusement as he answered. She climbed down the ladder with as much dignity as she could muster.

# Chapter Seven

Hennelyn went back to the tower twice the next day. The soldiers told her that she was so far the only one the bunji would accept food from, and it made her feel inordinately important. Though she felt that she had made progress with the bunji, she knew that he was not telling her all that he could, even with his limited grasp of the language. In fact, he had not told her much at all, except for unimportant aspects of his culture, with much gesturing. She went down to supper for the first meal with her family later that day, feeling discouraged. She knew her father would probably want a report, but she had nothing new to tell him.

The four of them talked about inconsequential things over the meal, while Hennelyn waited for the inevitable questions. But it wasn't until dessert came that anyone asked her anything. Strangely enough, it was Lisha who started the ball rolling. She nudged Hennelyn with her elbow and inquired, "What's wrong, young mistress? You are not eating your dessert. It's your favorite, you know; apple tart."

"Oh, yes," Hennelyn noted, taking a bite. It was good as always, sweet apple spiced with cinnamon.

"I think my little girl is finding how difficult it can be to get what one wants out of a captive. Isn't that right, Hennelyn?" her father observed.

She frowned in irritation.

"Well, I've learned more than the soldiers did," she retorted.

"Yes... about the way these bunjis fish and hunt, and what they do for sport. But have you learned anything about where they are all hiding? Do you know where to find their Adon Miru? Or anything about their sacred writings?"

"No," said Hennelyn slowly, "but I did find out that they have no intention of stopping their ambushes or leaving this country without resisting us. Oh yes, and the soldiers tell me that when I'm not there, the prisoner spends a lot of time kneeling on the floor under the window, staring out at the sky."

Tai leaned forward, with keen interest in his face.

"For what purpose?"

"I don't know," Hennelyn shrugged. "Maybe he's praying."

"Ah! But to whom? I have been briefed on what Starkhons say they believe. I wonder what this bunji would be able to tell us about it."

"I could try to find that out."

"Mmm," murmured Tai. "Perhaps it's time to try more serum after all."

"Father, you can't do that! It'll spoil all that I'm trying to do if you start sticking darts into him again. We'll be right back where we started."

"Well, we could hide the serum in the ale. It takes longer to get the effect of it that way, but it's a possibility."

"No it isn't, Father!" Hennelyn cried, red spots appearing high on her cheeks.

Tai gave her a silent, grim stare. He pointed out quietly, "I could be wrong, but I thought we were supposed to be working together on this. We do want the same thing, don't we, Henna?"

She dropped her eyes uncomfortably. "Of course. But let me explain. He will only eat if I bring something to him. If he finds that I have brought him drugged food or drink, I'll lose the little trust he has in me, and that will make me useless."

"I do believe the child is right," put in Jaero Lite, pleased. "I'm glad to see that my lessons have been of some help, after all."

"All right, Hennelyn," agreed Tai. "I'll give you two more days with him. But after that, if I still don't have the results I want, I'm doing things my way. Agreed?" After a moment Hennelyn nodded reluctantly. But the events of the following day completely upset their careful plans.

Hennelyn had barely finished breakfast with the prisoner the next morning before Solit Overon and Hennelyn's trainer Ghundrew came to take him to the house, per her father's orders. Naturally she followed along, full of curiosity. What did her father want with the captive bunji?

They trudged through the snow, the bunji barely keeping his feet under him between the two guards as Hennelyn followed behind, the crystal clouds of their breath lit by the bright morning sun.

As Ghundrew knocked, another soldier opened the door for them, and they stamped the snow off their feet before going inside. Hennelyn closed the door behind her, blinking as she waited for her eyes to adjust to the dimmer interior.

Then she saw. Her father sat in his usual seat near the fire. In front of him stood a small figure, just a little taller than their captive, with a soldier right behind.

This new bunji, dressed in white furs, turned his face towards them as they entered. Hennelyn could now see well enough in the light filtering through the eastern windows. What she saw gave her a start. His complexion was not the smooth brown of their captive but seemed reddish, as though he sported a permanent sunburn under his wrinkles. His eyes were much lighter brown as well, and his long hair was mostly grey with age. Yet where the color had not faded, it looked auburn. He leaned on a gnarled walking stick.

The older bunji looked relieved as he caught sight of the young captive. The younger bunji reacted much more violently. He cried out something in their bunji tongue and tried to run to his companion, except that the soldiers would not let him. He struggled to escape, but it was of little use. The old bunji took one step in his direction, brought effectively to a stop by his own guard's restraining hand. He contented himself with voicing some words loudly to the boy.

"Father, what's happening?" Hennelyn asked, moving a little further into the room.

Tai stood to his feet. "We have a visitor, my girl. It seems he walked right up to the Outpost gate with one of our perimeter patrols - just gave himself up."

"But why?" Tai shrugged.

"Ask him yourself."

"Can you speak to me in this language?" Hennelyn asked, coming closer to the newcomer.

"I can," he replied in a husky voice.

"Then tell us why you have come."

He croaked, "I have come to offer myself in the place of that youth you have taken. Let him go, and I will be your captive."

His fluency surprised Hennelyn, and his accent was slight. She had no trouble understanding.

"Quite an offer, isn't it, my girl! Well, old one, tell us what you can give us that we can't get from the boy."

The older bunji turned back to Tai.

"I don't know, for I cannot say what you want from him, sir. But he cannot speak the talk of the Tall People well. You see, I am different from most of the bunjis here. That is because I was born over the mountains, very far west where the ocean lies. We know this language there very well, for we have dealings with the Sun People often on the coasts. My grandfather was the first to welcome a ship of theirs into our harbors, when I was still a little child."

Tai seemed deep in thought for a minute.

"Are there bunjis then, all the way from here to the coast?" he asked at last.

"Yes, many different tribes. But not so many right here. Here are only those who have fled the east where your people have settled. There are many more of us west of the Kurin mountains." He paused. "Will you accept me then, Laero, and let the boy go? He is little more than a child."

Tai sat down again, chin resting on his hand. "Don't call me 'Laero.' We have no laeros here. I am General Kanow."

The bunji respectfully inclined his head. "General Kanow, sir."

"Are you the 'Laero' of this tribe?" Tai asked.

"No."

"Are you a leader of any kind?"

"Yes. I am a Luer."

"Am I supposed to know what that means?"

"I am one of the council of twelve under our Laero – our leader."

Tai looked towards the two soldiers flanking the prisoner.

"Take the prisoner back to the tower!" he ordered.

"Sir, yes, sir!"

Overon and Ghundrew saluted smartly and dragged the unhappy prisoner off as he protested loudly and incomprehensibly. Feeling strangely deflated, Hennelyn followed them out through the door. Obeying a sudden impulse, she stopped just outside, leaving the door open a crack so that she could listen.

She heard the old bunji protest, "You do not take my offer, sir? Why?"

"You are neither the Laero nor the Adon Miru. That means you are worth nothing to me. This is what I want, old one. I want you to tell your leader that my people are here to stay. Our emperor has sent us here to add these lands to his empire. Your people must surrender to us and come under our governance. You must stop ambushing our supply lines. Tell your Laero that I want to talk to your Adon Miru. He is the only one to whom we will state our terms."

The bunji answered, "Our people will not let him come. We have heard what has happened to the Adon Miru of the eastern bunjis - the simk tribe. And his apprentice. Now this Adon Miru born to the melan tribe is the only one left nearby."

"Do your people love their children, old one?" Tai asked in a dangerously quiet tone that made Hennelyn shiver.

There was a pause and then her father went on, "Very well, then, it looks like you have a job to do. You must make your Adon Miru understand that he has two days to come to me to hear my terms and agree to them."

"He will not surrender all of us and our sacred places here for the sake of one youth," the bunji rasped hoarsely.

"He has two days to decide," Tai said with grim finality. "After that, we will begin to send the boy back to you - one piece at a time. Do you understand?"

Hennelyn gasped, clapping her hand over her mouth to stifle the sound.

Her father went on, "Solit Kondar, escort this bunji out all the way to the gate. Tell the guards there that he is free by my order, to take a message to his people for me."

"Sir, yes, sir!"

Hearing the soldier's tramp and the bunji's shuffle nearing the door, Hennelyn scuttled away, rounding the far corner just before the soldier threw the door open and marched the bunji out into the compound. She peeked around the log walls and followed their progress, hailed by the barking dogs in the kennel, until she saw the gate swing shut behind the old bunji. The soldier headed for the barracks, and the dogs subsided.

She slumped back against the wall, trembling, unshed tears shining in her blue eyes. But no one saw. After a bit, she rose and walked slowly away.

At lunchtime, Hennelyn went up through the trapdoor in the tower for the second time that day. She arrived at the second level to see that the captive had been tied hand and foot, lying in a heap near the fireplace.

"Oh, can't you men leave the bunji alone?" she flared at the solit there.

"I had to get him up the ladder somehow, miss," the solit answered defensively. "He might not look it, but he's pretty slippery when he's angry and desperate. He fought us hard, the little..." he choked back the word he had intended to use.

"Well, cut him loose. I've brought his lunch." She indicated the basket she carried.

"I'll let you free him, if you don't mind, Mistress Hennelyn. He's not getting another crack at my fingers."

She took the basket over to the bunji and set it down. Taking out her own dagger, she sliced at the knotted cords around his wrists and ankles until they parted and fell off. The bunji laid still for the operation, then immediately rolled away from her and sprang up onto his feet. With a black look at the soldier, he let loose a string of angry utterances in his own tongue, rubbing at his wrists as he did so.

"Did you hear him, miss? Those are fighting words, if I'm not mistaken," the soldier observed darkly. "You just come over here, you little imp, and I'll let you have something you won't soon forget!"

The bunji could not have understood the Starkhon words, but he found the intent behind them clear enough. His black eyes flashed and, incredibly, he tried to push past Hennelyn to face up to the soldier. She flung an arm out into his path.

"That's enough! Stop it, both of you!" she commanded in the trade tongue. She reached out for the bunji, but he whirled around abruptly and strode to the fireplace with his back towards them both. His shoulders rose and fell with his breath. The solit shrugged and sat in the chair with a show of indifference.

"Whatever you say, miss," he answered in the same language.

Hennelyn sat down on the hearth of the fireplace, bringing the basket and resting it on her knees. She looked up at the bunji's profile, but he continued to frown into the cold ashy grate, ignoring her. She watched the anger slowly die out of his face, then he looked only worried and afraid.

"I'm sorry," was all that she could find to say. Finally his eyes dropped to her face.

"Where is he?" the bunji asked with concern.

"Who? Oh - you mean the other bunji. We let him go. He should be safe by now," Hennelyn told him.

"Let him go?"

"Yes, he's gone."

The bunji's eyes narrowed in suspicion.

"Not true!" he accused sharply.

"It is true. We sent the other bunji away with a message for your Laero." But her head lowered as she remembered the latter parts of her father's 'message.'

Her focus came back to the room with a start to see that the bunji was studying the top of her bowed head. He might have believed her words and felt better for it, but he still feared for his own fate.

"When can I go away?" he whispered wistfully.

"I don't know," she answered quietly. "Soon, I think."

She glanced towards the soldier and added in a louder tone, "Here, let's eat lunch. I've brought all your favorite things."

After a pause, a small smile ghosted his lips. He turned around and sat down next to her, ready to share the lunch.

His appetite was not as good as usual, but Hennelyn could understand that after the morning he'd had. When they had finished eating together, he regarded her expectantly. He was most likely wondering what questions she would have for him today.

But Hennelyn didn't have the heart to start any conversation. Whenever she looked at him, she thought of her father's threat. Each of the general's words sank like stones cast into a well, settling deep into her mind.

The young bunji's face was smooth and unblemished except for the bruise, his eyes large and expressive. His black hair was thick and as straight as an arrow. She noticed how the lobes of his small oval ears showed under the short haircut. *Would Father start with those?* she wondered. Her throat tightened: she knew from experience that Tai was equally dependable in both his promises *and* his threats.

As she struggled with her dark thoughts, the bunji seemed to understand that there was something wrong. He looked around restlessly; for what, she didn't know. Then his face brightened. He pulled something from the fourth finger of his broad left hand. It was a ring, just a thin gold circle with a clear blue stone fixed to the top of it. When he had been brought in, he'd been stripped down in the search for a weapon. Yet this ring had been overlooked. He held it up and seemed to compare it to the color of her eyes. With a satisfied nod, he grasped her hand and slipped it onto her middle finger.

She held the ring up for examination. The blue stone was not faceted, only polished, so that it did not sparkle. It gleamed cobalt, like a pebble underwater. There were darker veins of navy forking through it.

She took it off, but the bunji would not let her give it back. By gestures he made her understand that he was giving it to her, presumably to make her feel better. It astonished Hennelyn to think that this creature, who had no idea what would happen to him next in the hands of cruel giants, would make such a kind gesture to help her feel better. There was something very different about these little people.

68

Suddenly she asked, "That man in your fire-pictures. Who is it? What is his name?"

The bunji gave no answer besides a puzzled look. With a profound disappointment that surprised her, she realized that he didn't understand her.

Deep inside, Hennelyn felt a shift, a slipping of the tectonic plates of her soul. She loved her father, and her love had not diminished today, in spite of everything. But somehow her heart was turning towards a new view, one unanticipated and strange; it seemed to be the opposite of her father's and all that she had been raised to believe, all because of her short acquaintance with one young bunji.

*Yet how can I oppose my own father?* She didn't know, only that it felt right.

She heartily wished that Arcmas was around to discuss all of this with. *And yet… yes. There is still Nik.*

# Chapter Eight

**Letter from Arcmas - November:**

*Hi Hennelyn. Here in Glott, we are all in training, no matter the weather. I am under Cenetenor Jakhron, along with the other ninety-nine young men. We all sleep together in big barracks and eat in the mess halls. There are fireplaces in the barracks, but many of the boys are cold at night, and there have been cases of frostbite. I am glad that I have feathers, I don't feel the cold.*

*We have free time after the evening meal, but everyone avoids me. At first the officers wouldn't let me fly anywhere, but after a week or so, they allowed me an hour every evening. What else is there to do after supper? My only real company is owls.*

*The country here is flatter and much barer of trees than there, even compared to Khuntz. There are quite a few game animals. Right now everything is just an endless plain of snow, much more than we see at the Outpost. Plus no melts between cold days.*

*I thought Echthus trained me hard, but this is harder. When will they learn that I cannot march drills or run? I can only keep up if I use my wings to push me along. At least my archery is improving, and I've learned to use some different hand-to-hand combat moves. But training under Echthus was more fun. The other boys aren't sure whether to fear me or hate me, I think.*

*I've seen bunjis closer up in Khuntz and Glott. First ones I've seen that are not out in the wild. They seem to all be in service to Starkhon families. I haven't seen any just out on their own, and they don't seem to have homes to themselves. I haven't seen any bunji children. Starkhon children come to the base all the time to visit their brothers, and they are all over town when we come for supplies. Yet even there, I see no bunji children. I wonder where they are.*

*I had better stop writing. The boys near me want me to put my candle out.*

The evening of that momentous day, Hennelyn and Nik sat outside behind the stables, where the sinking sun had last rested on the wooden wall and imprinted a little residual warmth. They had not seen each other very much since Hennelyn had been so busy with the new prisoner.

Their breath smoked in the cold dark air as they sat wrapped up in furs. The bank of clouds above them looked abruptly sheared off as though cut with a knife, creating a dark, woolly arch of perfect symmetry beyond which the first stars winked out. Hennelyn and Nik knew that this strange formation would soon bring a balmy breeze, and the weather would warm until water dripped and ran like a spring thaw, even though it was December.

Nik's complaints about the cold stopped when Hennelyn described the events of the last few days and what her father had said to the old bunji.

"Wow. That's really unlaced," he finally said. "I mean, all of us in the servant's hall were wondering. We were really surprised that the older bunji was allowed to leave; now I know why."

"Yes."

"He was really brave to come here in the first place and offer himself up like that."

Nik glanced over at his friend, but couldn't see her face very well in the minimal light reflected from the snow.

"What will you do, Henna?" he wondered. "When... when the bunji's time runs out. Are you going to be there?"

She shivered at the thought of it. "No!"

Nik nodded. "Good. I wouldn't be able to stand it either. But maybe the Adon Miru will give himself up first."

Hennelyn turned to stare at him. "No, what I mean is, I won't be there - and the prisoner isn't going to be, either!"

Nik turned toward her. "What is that supposed to mean? You're not making any sense."

Hennelyn murmured, "I am not going to just sit and wait to see if the Adon Miru comes, or - or hope for some kind of bunji rescue attempt. I'm going to break the prisoner out myself!"

Nik gasped. "Are you crazy? You don't know what you're saying! You're - you're talking treason!"

"I know, but..."

"Shhhh!" he hissed, staring around. She could see the whites of his wide eyes even in the low light. When Nik was satisfied no one could possibly overhear them, he went on quietly, "Besides, how would you do it?"

"I have some ideas."

"I don't want to know anymore! Just in case they ask me about it at your trial. I don't believe this, Hennelyn - you're just a kid! Not to mention the daughter of a general."

"No one will know it was me. They won't even guess it was. Because it's me. Understand?"

"No I don't," he sulked.

Hennelyn sighed. "Maybe if you met the bunji, like I have, you would."

"Hennelyn, I feel sorry for him. You know I do. But I am more concerned about you. And have you considered what might happen to your father?"

A long silence fell. Nik showed his agitation by continuously rubbing his deerskin trousers with his hands. Finally Hennelyn reached out and clapped her hand over one of his to stop it.

"Nik, I'm sorry. I don't know what I can tell you. I just know that I couldn't live with myself if I don't help the prisoner."

Nik could only shake his head. "I don't know what to think, Henna. I think this is a really bad idea. If it goes wrong, you're the one who could die. And it would be a traitor's death. Did you think of that, Henna?"

"Yes. I did."

"When are you planning your – your prison break?" His tone sounded pained.

"Tomorrow night. Late. Nik, you've told me lots of times how you hate some of the things Starkhons do. But I'm doing the right thing now – aren't I?"

"I don't know," he murmured. "I'm afraid for you." He reached out and gave her a clumsy hug before standing up. For a moment he gazed down at her, shoulders slumped. Then he crept carefully, quietly away.

After a few minutes, Hennelyn stood up and returned to the house. She wanted her own room and a hot fire, and she needed to think.

In the end, Hennelyn's plan was elegant in its simplicity. Since the security for their fortress was all concentrated on the wall around it, and patrols were posted beyond the town against bunjis trying to get in, they didn't particularly watch for anyone getting out. Security inside the walls was practically nil. She believed that if she was caught walking around outside, she could plead insomnia and the need for a post-midnight stroll. Then she would try again the following night. But she hoped she could free the bunji tomorrow night.

Even with her night's sleep reduced by half because of her plotting, Hennelyn still woke early the next morning. No one seemed over eager to talk over breakfast. Perhaps everyone was waiting for something to happen.

"Has there been any movement, any bunjis seen outside the walls, sir?" Jaero Lite asked at last.

Tai's gaze snapped to the tutor. He had been staring at his daughter in puzzlement most of the morning.

"No, no sign of them," he answered shortly.

"Do you think they will give up their Adon Miru?"

"I don't know. The old bunji said not. But they have until the day after tomorrow. And the patrols are ready to pick up any bunji they see."

Tai's dark eyes centred again on Hennelyn.

"Are you going to feed the prisoner again today, my girl?"

With a start she answered, "Well yes, Father, but not until lunchtime. I was going to visit Wingfoot for a little while this morning. Am I still excused from lessons today?"

"Yes, of course. If you wish. But you know that we have given up on interrogation for now; the boy cannot speak well enough. And our plans have changed, anyway. I just wondered how you were… handling this. My men have told me you may be feeling, well, a bit of an affinity for the prisoner. You know… some sympathy."

His gaze probed into hers as he spoke, a small line etched between his brows.

Hennelyn held back a strong urge to kick herself. Of course! Her father was expecting her to have heard about his words yesterday; he could see that she was not acting like herself.

Trying to inject some pathos into her voice, she asked, "Father, do you really mean to do… what you said?" That's good, she thought. I sound like I don't really believe it.

"It probably won't come to that. They have two days, and I think the bunjis will knuckle under."

"You think they will. But… what if they don't?"

"They will. If not before, then certainly the day after the deadline."

Lisha smothered a gasp. Now Hennelyn did not have to play act; her gorge suddenly rose and she swallowed it down with an effort.

Tai spoke to the Luinians as much as to his daughter as he stated flatly, "I am a general. I am answerable to Emperor Tol Lorsumn, and to his ambassador Siras Thraulor. I will do what it takes to succeed, and if that means-"

He broke off, waving an impatient hand.

"All of you have been so sheltered from the realities of military life up to now. All the time we lived in Flaethe, after my marriage, I only had trade relations duties with the Luinians. And afterward, in Kuntz - merely a desk job! But now I am in command once more, and I will command. How do you suppose I became a general in the first place? As Starkhons, we conquer and we dominate. We are feared. It is what glorifies the emperor and makes our empire great."

"Or maybe it just makes us bullies," muttered Hennelyn. But she could see by his scowl that she had gone too far. Even Jaero Lite and Lisha looked shocked.

"I'm sorry, Father," she quickly apologized.

He dropped his cutlery with a clatter; his chair scraped jarringly over the stone floor as he abruptly stood.

"We'll talk about it later! I have work to do."

He stomped up the stairs to his office in the loft. Hennelyn sighed ruefully to herself. At least she had allayed her father's suspicions. Still, she hadn't meant to blurt that out, especially as it was exactly how she felt now.

Jaero Lite a-hemmed delicately. "I, too, have work to do. Lessons to plan for you, young lady. When Longest Night is over, we two will have much study to do together."

He got up as well and went to his ground floor room under the loft.

As the servants came to the table and Lisha made signs of leaving, Hennelyn stopped her. It was time to get the first thing she needed for her plans, and it was in Lisha's room. When the Luinian stood up, she suddenly asked, "Lisha, could I speak to you for a moment? About Mother?"

Lisha's drawn face relaxed into a smile.

"I was just about to ask you if you needed to talk, mistress. In my chamber?"

"Sure." The sound of clattering dishes followed them until Lisha shut the door of her chamber. It was west of Jaero's and situated right under Hennelyn's own loft bedroom, sharing the same fireplace chimney.

Lisha's chamber was a little bigger than Hennelyn's but just as roughly made. In it hung the only portrait in the place. It was a painting of Hennelyn's mother, Raethena, as she had been soon after her marriage to Tai. She had only been thirty-six when she died, having given her older husband only one child, a daughter.

"I don't look much like her, do I?" Hennelyn remarked.

In the portrait, Raethena's white-blonde hair was braided up onto her head, twining around it. This showed off her slender, well-shaped neck. Her painted azure eyes were large with sprays of light lashes like Hennelyn's, and they seemed to glimmer with life. Her small, pink bow of a mouth curved in a close-lipped impish smile in her oval face, while Hennelyn had inherited the stronger jaw and fuller lips of her father. The portrait portrayed her mother to the shoulders, draped in a sunset pink dress which belled out from the upper arms and left a modest half circle of her white bosom bare. On her flawless skin gleamed a necklace, an exquisite sliver of mother-of-pearl shaped like a heart and carved on its surface with the lines of an unfamiliar flower. Raethena had been small and graceful, but her daughter was going to grow tall, and her broader frame had already acquired more athletic muscle. Yes, I am my father's daughter in more ways than one, she thought.

"You may not look much like her, but you *are* like her," Lisha replied.

"How do you mean?"

"She, too, would have had compassion on the little bunji prisoner."

"Oh, that."

"Yes, *that*. It's alright to pity him, Hennelyn. I do."

"What good is pity? It can't help him."

The girl twisted her hair impatiently round her hand. "I wonder what Mother would have done? Would she have been able to help? Lisha, did... did Father love her so much that she could have changed his mind?"

"I don't know," Lisha answered hesitantly. "But I do know heloved her. You were too young to see how her death affected him. It was like... part of him died too. It was for his sake as much as yours that Jaero Lite and I left Flaethe for this northern place, with your maid Dewdra and Follamo's family as well. We were all part of Raethena's household; she had noble blood, you know. And what else could we have done?" she said. "He was her husband."

"Noble blood," Hennelyn murmured, though she had heard this many times before. "And they met at a ball at a trade negotiation."

"Yes. Starkhons wanted the help of the Luinians to acquire some of the goods they needed up here in the north."

"And everyone was surprised when they got married."

Lisha laughed merrily. Hennelyn used that moment to sidle closer to the governess's bedside table.

"Everyone!" Lisha agreed. "Your father was bold and dashing; wild by our standards, and already a general by the age of thirty. He was sent to us, I think, because he was a good negotiator, and his superiors thought he would be able to squeeze as much from us as possible. But as I recall, I don't think he was ever less than fair. Of course, the family was against the marriage."

"But Mother married him anyway, and tamed him."

"Tamed him?" Lisha repeated in surprise. "No, no, I would never say she tamed him. Gentled him maybe, for a little while. They were happy together, but I don't think he liked those twelve years in Flaethe. Your father was made for adventure; I think he missed all the action he was used to. He wanted to be a part of the conquest of this land."

"And now he is," murmured Hennelyn.

Lisha's eyes transmitted dismay. "Yes. And you and Arcmas are in the thick of it now too, through no fault of your own." She paused. "I… I think that you should stop visiting the bunji now, Hennelyn. I don't want you to see things you aren't old enough to…to…"

"Don't worry, Lisha," Hennelyn reassured her gently. "I will stay away when I need to. But you never know – maybe the bunji will tell me something today that will change things."

But the woman looked doubtful.

"Lisha?"

"Yes, dear?"

"Can I look at Mother's dress again? Maybe I will fit it now."

The Luinian woman's face brightened.

"Yes, of course! Especially since we may need to alter it for your coming-of-age in April. Just a moment!"

She moved quickly to the trunk at the foot of her bed, a beautifully carved piece of dark wood, brass-bound, that had once been Raethena's. As she lifted the lid and rummaged through it, Hennelyn quickly plucked a skin pouch from Lisha's bedside table and dumped some of its contents into her own little pouch, produced from her tunic pocket. How much? How much? She had seen Lisha use these powders but she didn't precisely know how much was too much. She took an amount she believed would work on two men.

By the time Lisha had unwrapped and pulled out the flowing

pink dress, Hennelyn was done. She spent a few more minutes in the room as Lisha fussed and measured the dress on her body, but she was anxious to leave. A few minutes later, she did.

Her next stop was the stables. There was one soldier inside, pitching hay for the few horses that were lucky enough to be in residence, but he didn't notice Hennelyn enter. She grabbed a slightly withered fall carrot from the bucket to offer to Wingfoot. He came to the half-door of his stall to greet her with a friendly blow. She fed him the snack and rubbed the white spot on his nose, but her eyes mostly studied the man. When she was sure she was unobserved, she went quickly to the wall in the next empty stall and pulled down a length of rope. She took off her heavy coat and hung the coil around her body, putting the coat back on over it.

She peered round the post of the empty stable to see the soldier poke his pitchfork in the haystack and exit the building. Then she also crept out, back to the house.

Jaero Lite was standing in the great hall, spreading either a map or some other large paper out on the table, in front of the low fire.

"Hello, Hennelyn. Are you planning to eat lunch with us today?"

"No sir! I am about to go to the kitchens to order lunch for the prisoner."

"I see."

"Where is Father?"

"I believe he is out looking over the building site. If a real melt sets in, they may continue working."

He turned back to his project. There were musical sounds emanating from Lisha's room. Practicing, apparently. Hennelyn ran up to her own room, slid the rope under her bed, replaced her coat, and came down again. She passed Jaero Lite once more on her way out.

Outside, she noticed that the weather was warming up, just as last night's cloud formation had predicted. Soon she would not need her heavy coat – a light jacket would do. She wasn't sure if a melt right now would be a help or a hindrance to her plans. She wasn't even sure of her plans, for that matter, but she was committed now.

The large kitchen was as warm as usual when Hennelyn entered it. The shutters on the building were all standing open because of the many fires burning inside, cooking food for everyone in the compound. The staff who prepared the food cycled regularly through all the Starkhon farmers, but Hennelyn was familiar with all of them. They all greeted her respectfully, and she nodded back. She was a frequent visitor there, and all of them loved to give her special treats.

Today she noted with interest that one table was covered with strips of wild game jerky. No wonder, since it was a spiced treat especially made for the Longest Night holiday. And it was salty too. Quite spicy and salty. This was a stroke of luck! She filed the information away for later.

When no one was looking, she surreptitiously palmed a small sharp knife from the table. One of the women walked over to hand her the basket containing lunch, both for Hennelyn and the prisoner. She thanked the woman and took it.

When she entered the tower this time, the bunji regarded her reproachfully. She reasoned that he had missed her at breakfast. Yes, there was the uneaten, lumpy porridge once again, cold and unappetizing. Why the solits insisted on bringing it was a mystery to her.

When she approached the prisoner, he did not even try to moderate his voice.

"My friend... come back? I go away now?" he asked eagerly.

She shook her head. "No, I'm sorry. Not yet."

"But why? I am..." He spread his arms as if to indicate that he had nothing to offer "Why?" he repeated.

"You *know* why," she said. "They want to exchange you for the Adon Miru." He only looked confused. They sat down together on the hearth. Hennelyn held her hands up in front of him, tips of the fingers pointing heavenward. She wiggled one hand.

"Adon Miru."

With the other, she pointed at him and wiggled it.

"You."

Then she moved her hands to indicate one replacing the other. She saw comprehension dawn in his black eyes. Then he shook his head.

"No. No. Not Adon Miru. Not come here," he said emphatically.

"Where is the Adon Miru? We only want to talk to him," she told him, wincing a little over the lie. "Can you tell us where to find him?"

The bunji only returned her stare and said nothing. She switched topics.

"How old are you?"

"I am alive nineteen... summers."

"What is your name?" Silence.

She continued, "I am Hennelyn. You are..." Still nothing.

Apparently he understood but chose not to tell her. *Alrighty then.*

"Well, whoever you are, this is how it is: the Adon Miru either comes here to us – or you never leave. Ever. Do you understand?"

After a pause, the bunji nodded grimly.

"So, where can we find the Adon Miru?" No answer. She balled up her fists next to her temples in frustration.

"Oh, by the emperor – do you want to die?!" she burst out.

Now, at last, she saw a flicker behind his eyes - she dared to hope she'd gotten through. One more try.

"I know you can tell me if you want to. Where is the Adon Miru?"

Her new, tender shoot of hope withered when he sat back and crossed his arms stubbornly.

"I don't understand your people!" she cried in despair. "Do they all think the Adon Miru is more important than you are? Is there no one out there who wants to save you?" Taking a deep breath, she went on, "I am trying to help you. What about your family? Is there no one who wants you to come home in one piece? You have one day left for that. One day."

At that, the bunji's eyes developed a damp sheen. Blinking, he struggled to find the right words.

"Want me home... yes. But Adon Mirus will not come here. They are too important, yes."

Hennelyn felt an inner shock.

"What do you mean, they will not come?" she blurted out. "Are there more than one Adon Miru near here? Are there – are there two?" She glanced at the attending solit, who was naturally avidly listening, because it was his job. He gave her a half-salute of victory. The bunji realized what he'd let slip and closed his eyes in anguish.

Even though Hennelyn had not exactly been trying to elicit this new information, she still felt a stab of remorse. Hadn't she just shown herself to be a cunning Starkhon interrogator, worthy of acclaim? No matter that the bunji was alone, vulnerable, and terrified for his life. *Siras Thraulor would probably give me a medal if he knew,* she thought.

Sickened, she jerked up onto her feet. Her appetite was gone; she just wanted out of there. The bunji rose to his feet as well. As she turned to go, he spoke to her softly.

"Goodbye... Sunchild."

She turned back.

"No. No, it isn't goodbye. Not yet. I won't leave you all alone here. I will be back at suppertime." She hoped he felt a little reassured. But she couldn't get down the ladder fast enough.

She drew a bit of comfort from one, vital fact: she still had time to rescue him.

# Chapter Nine

There were a few hours to kill before supper; she was restless. She took Wingfoot out of his stall and spent some time putting him through his paces around the inside of the compound wall. Soldiers were moving about doing their chores. It was cloudy outside, but the air continued to warm considerably throughout the day. It felt like spring, but the trees never seemed to be fooled by these midwinter warm spells. Somehow they grasped that a great deal of winter was left to be endured.

As she practiced her tricks, she caught a glimpse of Nik near one of the buildings, helping his father and little brothers chink up holes in the half-log walls of the barracks. He stood up and watched her until she was out of his sight.

Finally, supper hour arrived, and she went back to the tower. She had the usual basketful of food, but it contained extras, pieces of the festival jerky. She handed some to the solit on the ground floor who let her in. A different man since lunchtime. She knew this one's name.

"Here, for you, Solit Drakhor," she said, offering him a generous amount of the jerky. "A Longest Night treat for our faithful soldiers. I noticed they had it ready in the kitchens."

He seemed surprised.

"Thank you, Mistress Hennelyn."

She eyed the tin pitcher of water on the table as she approached the ladder. It was about half full. *Excellent.*

Drakhor climbed up to unlatch the trap door for her. She stepped up slowly, encumbered with her basket, and offered the same treat to the soldier up there. This one was Solit Nakhanor. She recognized him; he had a white streak in the black hair that waved back from his forehead. Not from age, he had explained to her once, but because of a head wound he had suffered some years ago.

After he had thanked her, Nakhanor nodded at the bunji, who was kneeling on the floor facing the window. The shutters were open to let in the warmer breeze.

"I was told when I came for my shift that he has been like that all afternoon – since you left."

Hennelyn slowly approached the prisoner, and stood over him.

His eyes were open, but he only gave her a glance before returning his gaze to the scudding grey clouds - free to blow wherever they wished, while he was not. Hennelyn sank down next to the bunji. She did not bother to ask him anything. What was there to say? After a moment, she reached out to take his hand. He allowed her that.

If Nakhanor was hoping to hear interesting revelations like the previous solit, he was bound to be disappointed. Hennelyn and the bunji did not speak at all. After a bit, she leaned in close and whispered into his ear. Immediately he came out of his funk enough to show interest in the supper, so the two of them ate together in silence. Then she rose and started to gather up the things she had not cleared away earlier when she had left in such haste, from the cold porridge to the empty lunch basket, plus the supper basket. He gave her one short glance over his shoulder, saw the solit watching, and quickly turned forward again.

But the whispering had piqued Nakhanor's interest. He knocked for Drakhor to unlatch the trap door, and as they waited, he inquired of Hennelyn, "What did you tell him there at the end?"

She made her eyes open wide and innocent. "Oh… I just told him that everything would be alright."

"For tonight, anyway," the solit quipped.

"Yes. For tonight."

She started to toe her way down, clumsy with her two baskets.

"Goodnight, mistress," he told her disappearing head.

"Goodnight. Enjoy the jerky," her voice floated up. In a moment, she was on the ground floor.

When Drakhor climbed up to latch the trap, she quickly shook her pouch of powders into the water, then picked up the pitcher and swirled it around a bit. The level of the water had gone down slightly; maybe Drakhor had taken one drink. But both solits would probably empty it between them, to counteract the spices and salt of the jerky.

The pitcher was back in its spot, and she was already leaving as Drakhor came down again. He closed the door behind her. But on that door, she knew there was neither lock nor bar.

She leaned against it a moment and gave a great, shaky sigh. *So far, so good. Only one thing left to do.* If everything worked out as she planned, no one would ever discover that her quiet words to the prisoner had been, "I will be back later in the night. Don't drink the water!"

She sat at the table before bed, eating a snack. Her father joined her by the fire with a hot drink. From the smell of it, he had spiked it with zorkhta. That was unusual. Maybe he wasn't easy in his mind either.

"Hello, Father," she greeted him, "did you start any work on the new site today?"

"No. We won't unless there is a real melt, and the ground dries up a bit. Then we might put together some rafters... Hennelyn?"

"Yes, Father?"

"Solit Tranton informed me what the bunji told you - that there are *two* Adon Mirus in this region. Why didn't you report this earlier? It's a success, though a small one."

"Oh! Well, I... I knew that the solit would give you a report. I suppose it slipped my mind."

He seemed dubious, but his eyes were having trouble meeting hers anyway. At the moment, it was a good thing. She thought he might notice how tense she was if he looked at her more closely.

"I see. Two Adon Mirus – I wonder if it's true, and if so, why? I suppose one is the master and one the apprentice. I hope one of them shows up, at least, by tomorrow. Well, keep up the good work. One more day, if you're willing. Who knows what could happen?"

She shrugged, and gave a pale smile. "Who knows?"

After Hennelyn went to bed, she lay awake, listening to coyote song that rose and fell intermittently. Suddenly she startled awake from a half-sleep. She sat up in fright. How late was it? Too late? Or maybe too early. There was only one way to find out, and that was to get going.

She slipped out of bed, fully clothed, then knelt down and pulled the coil of rope from beneath her bed. She draped this over her shoulder and body. Over that, she put on her lighter fox coat and fastened it. Then she opened her door, crept through it, and tiptoed down the hall. She paused outside her father's door, believing she could hear him snoring. He often stayed awake until near midnight, so it must be later than that. Reassured, she went on her way.

The hall was dark, and the fire was a black mass shot through with pulsing orange veins. It had burnt down far but wasn't out. From that evidence she deduced that the time was right. She slipped outsideand east across the sticky snow of the compound. The night sky boasted no moon, but the snow illuminated things a bit. She slipped and fell but went on more carefully afterwards.

At the door of the tower, she hesitated for a moment. On a deep indrawn breath, she quickly pushed it open and slid inside. Her eyes fearfully swept the room, but in the low lantern-light she saw that Solit Drakhor was asleep in his chair, his upper body lying loosely on the table, arms akimbo. The fire was low; he had not been awake to bank it up. She moved to the ladder and climbed it quietly. Her heart jumped at a sudden sound from the man below. She relaxed when she recognized it as a choked snore.

She paused again just under the trap door. No sound above. She opened the catch of the trap door, and struggled to push it open – it was so heavy. It was going to fall! But no. The bunji's white fur-clad legs appeared and between the two of them they wrestled the door silently to the floor. There was a lantern up here as well, but the fire was burning higher. The bunji must have fed it by himself. She peered around for Nakhanor, and saw him sprawled back in his chair with his legs stretched out, his chin resting on his chest. He, too, breathed heavily in sleep. It struck her as a strange sight. She had never seen a Starkhon guard asleep on duty before – it just didn't happen. The penalties for such things were harsh.

Suddenly, she was enfolded in a strong, rabbit-furred hug. The bunji had dressed in his coat and boots again, which had been resting forgotten in a corner all this time. He was ready to go. He released her, and started for the ladder, but she pulled him away.

"But… I go home now. Yes?" he plaintively whispered.

"Not that way. Over here."

Hennelyn went to the window and unfastened the bottom part of the shutters. Since Nakhanor slept in the only chair, she recruited the bunji's help to hoist her up, knee on his shoulder, to undo the top bolts. It surprised her how easily he lifted her. Apparently he was much stronger than he looked.

She pulled the two wooden wings open. A breeze flowed in, chill but not frigid. She took off her coat with a small shiver and removed the rope she had brought, tying one end securely to an iron ring in the wall below the window, a ring opposite the one to which the bunji had once been chained.

It was a long rope, but she had her doubts that it would reach the entire twenty feet down to the ground. The bunji regarded her with silent intensity. He, too, looked somewhat doubtful.

"Come on, time to climb down," she told him quietly. When he didn't move, she added, "You can climb, can't you?"

With a reproachful look, he neared the window.

All of a sudden, Hennelyn remembered the two guards who would be making their way on opposite routes outside the walls below, each with a dog. She clapped a hand to her forehead, silently berating

herself for this huge oversight. Then she hurried to extinguish the
lantern, so that the lighted window could not be seen from outside. In
the eye-damping dark, she fumbled her way back to where the bunji
stood. At that moment, Nakhanor stirred and moaned. Hennelyn froze,
gripping the bunji's arm hard. The soldier subsided, and soon, so did
her heartbeat.

"Just a minute," she hissed. "Two guards outside."

She hitched herself up onto the windowsill so that she could
stare down at the ground below. She hung there a long minute, listening
and squinting as her eyes adjusted to the dark. She could see no moving
shadows against the snow or hear any crunching of boots below on the
recently melted and refrozen crust. But who knew? They could be right
around the corner.

She dropped lightly down again beside the bunji, staring into his
dim face.

"Two guards around the wall, with dogs," she whispered,
gesturing. "Night patrols out past the town. Understand? Can you go
around them all?"

His dark head nodded, shiny black against the matte black of
the darkness behind him. She offered him the skin mitts in her pockets,
and he put them on. All at once she remembered the knife she had
filched in the kitchen, and offered him that, too.

"In case you need to defend yourself," she told him. He took it
reluctantly and pocketed it somewhere in the mass of rabbit fur. Now
she bent to make a cradle with her hands for him to step into, but he
grasped her arm, peering into her face.

"You come, too?" he whispered. But she shook her head.

"Not today. But someday soon. You watch for me, and I will
come. You look for me."

She ringed her eyes with curled fingers to show him what she
meant. He paused, thinking, then slowly nodded again. He stepped
into her laced hands, and she boosted him with all her might up onto the
top of the sill. He nearly fell out from the force of her push but managed
to steady himself on the thick edge, gripping the rope. Hennelyn only
hoped he could make it down without breaking his neck. He stared
down at her.

"Go!" she whispered fiercely. "If you want to get out of here in
one piece, go now!" She waved him on.

"Brinkle," he said softly, splaying a gloved hand on his chest.

"What?"

"My... my name is Brinkle," he told her very clearly in his accented tones. He then grasped the rope in both hands and worked his way out over the drop, disappearing as he began to climb down the rope with admirable agility. Hennelyn hitched her elbows up onto the ledge again to watch as much of his progress as she could see. The scraping and thumps of his boots seemed loud to her, but at least the coyotes were still exercising their lungs to great effect. Suddenly she thought she heard a bark, not too far away. She watched and listened for a long time, her chest and arms beginning to ache from the strain. The sounds Brinkle was making ceased, and the rope went slack.

Soon after, she heard the dog bark again, closer, and the drumming of its feet as it ran up below the window. She could hear it snuffling, then moving a few feet away into the dark, whining softly. She let herself slip down off the ledge and froze beneath the window, heart hammering. But nothing else happened until a man's irritable voice called the dog back. The guard was now walking below her. She was glad that she had earlier doused the light.

Carefully she pulled the knot apart, and swiftly wound up the rope. It was dark out, but the guard might see it hanging there anyway if he looked close enough. After inching the shutters closed, she gasped in dismay. She had forgotten that she could no longer reach the upper shutter bolt, now that she was alone! Oh well. On second thought, she decided to leave the shutters open. Let them think what they would about that.

Now she had to get out of there and back to her room. She had a bad feeling that the changing of the prisoner's guards was imminent, not really knowing what hour of the night it was. She crept back through the dark night.

She was just at the corner of the house when a shadow detached itself and grabbed her, pressing a hand over her mouth. She barked a smothered cry into it and almost tried to flip her attacker, when it occurred to her that he was keeping unusually quiet. Heart thudding wildly, she stopped resisting until she was released, and then she turned around. Her breath whooshed out with relief when she saw the pale hair of Nik.

"Nik! What are you trying to do? Give me a heart attack?" She gave him a light punch that nevertheless rocked him on his feet.

"I was watching for you," he whispered reproachfully. "I couldn't sleep with worry. Is it too late to help you with this – this prison break?"

"Too late, yes. It's done!"

"Done already?" He sounded astonished. "Is he gone, then?"

"I don't know. I hope so. I didn't hear a sound out of the ordinary."

Nik sagged a little. "That's it, then. Nothing to do but weather the consequences," he observed glumly. A wave of annoyance washed over her.

"Look, do you want to help? Then here." She thrust the rope at him. "Go and put this rope back in the stable, in the stall next to Wingfoot. I was going to, but I don't know if there is still time, and if there isn't... I would have to burn it in my fireplace, I guess!"

Nik took it with reluctance, but said nothing.

Just then, a hundred feet away, they saw the door to the barracks open, and two soldiers came out with a lantern. The two children immediately flattened themselves against the wall of the house. Hennelyn's breath quickened. Shift change for the prisoner guard already! Her time was up.

The men talked quietly as they headed for the east tower, passing the children some distance away. They were too far for their lantern-light to reach, but as soon as they got to their destination, the alarm would be raised.

When the soldiers were far enough off, the children stood away from the wall.

"Don't worry, I'll take this back," Nik reassured her, brandishing the tell-tale rope. "You get back inside."

*No time to argue.* They parted company, Nik to the stable and Hennelyn sneaking back inside the house. She hurried as quietly as possible up to her chamber and took refuge inside. Now to undress for bed. Her fire had gone out, and it was icy under the coverlet when she climbed in. But the furs gathered and magnified her body heat, soon taking off the chill.

She lay tensely in her bed and listened hard for whatever came next. She could hardly believe that she had succeeded. Or maybe the bunji – Brinkle – would still be caught before morning. She hoped not. He may have been ready to give up his life for the Adon Mirus, but she didn't think he would hold on to the secret of their location for long under threat of torture. Her heart labored away, beyond her control to quiet it. For her, there was still a long night ahead.

# Chapter Ten

To her amazement, Hennelyn woke from a deep sleep when she first heard sounds in the house: her father's voice downstairs in the hall. She sat up quickly, listening, but the words were muffled by her closed door. She slid out of bed and opened the shutters of her window. The pearly grey light of early morning was just beginning to touch the white world outside. *Why hadn't the alarm been sounded? Surely they had discovered the escape hours ago.*

She pattered over to her door, bare feet slapping against the cool wood. Cracking it open and peeking out, she saw that her father had dressed and was speaking to some soldiers in the hall below the balcony. There stood Marshal Maraton and both centenors.

Hennelyn fumbled around in the half-light for her robe and slippers and pulled them on, shivering. She slipped out of her room and stood out of sight, listening.

"The searches have turned up nothing, General," Centenor Hernak reported.

"What about the two drugged guards?" Tai inquired.

Marshal Maraton answered, "Solit Nakhanor is just beginning to wake. The other cannot be roused."

"And how do you suppose the drug was administered?"

"We don't know yet."

"The water jug was empty," put in Centenor Stankhreed.

"Tell me your theory about how the prisoner got out, Marshal."

"I... I can't be sure, sir. Nakhanor was locked in, but the window shutters were open."

"Ridiculous!" blustered Maraton. "The bunji could not have jumped that distance without hurting himself! And how did he open the shutters? The top bolts were out of his reach. And where did he lay hands on a drug of any kind? In any case, he couldn't have put it in the pitcher when he was locked in the upper story!"

"Could another bunji have gotten into the compound, sir?" asked Hernak. "We all know they are sneaky little imps."

"Maybe. Perhaps that old bunji came here merely to do reconnaissance of the place," Tai proposed. "And one or more of them got back in tonight."

"But how? How would they get over the walls? And out of the tower – if that's the way they went? Are they some breed of wall-climbing insect?"

"With ropes," suggested Stankhreed. Hernak huffed at that.

"Then where are the ropes? They would have been left behind; ropes don't come down to you when you call them!"

"No, but it seems the most likely solution. If it isn't true, then the only possibility left is…"

"The prisoner had help from inside. There is a traitor in our midst," finished Tai grimly. They all fell silent. Just then, a board creaked under Hennelyn's foot where she had been drawn out to the railing of the balcony to hear better. All four men looked up.

"Hennelyn, my girl!" her father exclaimed as he caught sight of her, "I'm sorry; did we wake you?" His gaze was a bit evasive, as though he wondered how long she'd been listening.

"What's happened, Father?" she asked as innocently as possible.

"You will find out about it soon enough anyway, I suppose. The prisoner has escaped."

Hennelyn pretended to be just as astonished about it as they were.

"How? And when? I just saw him yesterday evening!"

"Hours ago. Before the night shift change. But how? Your guess is as good as ours. You did not see or hear anything unusual last night, did you, my girl?"

"No, Father."

She almost choked on the lie, but he nodded and flapped a hand.

"Go back to bed, Hennelyn. We are leaving for the barracks, and you need not be disturbed again until breakfast arrives. I will be in consultations most of the day, but we will talk later. Come along, men, on the double! We may as well wait out there for the troops to muster."

They all strolled to the door, donned their coats, and filed out after Tai.

After a moment, Hennelyn re-entered her room. Downstairs she heard Lisha and Jaero Lite come out and start talking softly but excitedly to each other. Of course they had been listening to everything from behind their own doors. She shuffled back to her bed and sat down. Her body started to tremble uncontrollably, so she clasped her hands tightly together under her knees until the spasm passed. It looked like she had succeeded in her plan, and a few hours' search in the night had turned up no clues.

*Thank goodness no one was found dead - especially Brinkle! Or some soldier he was forced to kill. But what am I to do now?* She'd thought she would be happy if her plan worked. But her father's words kept echoing in her head: *a traitor in our midst.*

Something trickled down her cheek. She put her finger to it and discovered, with dull surprise, a teardrop. More were trying to escape. She laid down on her bed, pulled the covers up over her head, and let them come. Finally, after the tears stopped, she slept again.

When she awoke a couple of hours later, it was to hear light and happy voices echoing through the building. A fire had at some point been lit in her room, and it was now comfortably warm. She dressed and came out to see Lisha, Jaero Lite, Dewdra, and three of Follamo's family putting up decorations. *Oh, of course. Longest Night celebrations begin the day after tomorrow.*

As she descended, they greeted her cheerfully, and Lisha remarked, "Child, you overslept breakfast! Shall I send Dewdra to find you some?"

"No, no," Hennelyn yawned. She didn't want them to fuss over her; or to be required to match their cheerful chatter. She wanted to talk only to Nik.

Lisha came near, and laid a hand on her cheek. "You look tired, dear. Of course, you were awake early this morning; I heard you speaking to your father. That was … some news this morning, wasn't it?"

"Yes!" Hennelyn agreed with false enthusiasm. "It was."

"Aren't you happy to know the bunji was rescued?" Lisha pressed. "We are!"

Hennelyn was saved from further comment by the interruption of Nik's little sister, Winellika, six years old and the only girl of the family.

"Mistress Hennelyn!" the child piped, rushing up and wrapping her small arms around the older girl.

"Hi, Nelly." Hennelyn picked her up, the little girl's white-blonde head dropping onto her shoulder. Her eight-year-old brother Wanskitero (nicknamed Skeet), stood back shyly, content to smile his greeting.

"Whoa, you're getting heavy, Nelly! Where's Nik?" Hennelyn asked. The reply came from Nelly's mother, Neesha, yet another slender Luinian blonde.

"He and his father and brother will be helping to lay wood out for all the buildings, young mistress. We will need extra for the holiday."

"Shall I fetch your breakfast for you, Mistress?" Dewdra kindly offered. "I lit the fire in your room earlier, but you didn't wake."

"No, that's all right. I'll eat in the kitchen," Hennelyn hedged. She set Nelly down.

"And then you will return and help us with decorating?" Jaero Lite asked. "We know how you enjoy it."

His tone rang a little false to her ears. She sensed that they, like herself, were trying too hard not to miss Arcmas on this first major holiday without him.

"Sure, I will."

The kitchen was warm and bustling, as usual; kettles boiling, dishes being washed. Windows stood open to tempt the spring-warm breeze inside. The farmers on kitchen duty greeted Hennelyn with the usual respect. On her request, one of them fixed her some scrambled eggs with cheese on toasted bread.

She ate contentedly. The kitchen was noisy but cheerful, and no one pestered her to talk to them, since they were busy with their work. Clean-up from breakfast and preparations for lunch went on all at the same time. Two hundred soldiers and the General's household were a lot to feed.

She drank her milk and waited expectantly. Finally her patience was rewarded. Nik and his ten-year-old brother entered with a wagon full of wood. They stacked it up near the stoves and fireplace. Nik's eyes picked her out immediately, snapping magnetically onto hers. Their shared secret created almost a current between them before they broke their gaze.

A moment later, Nik and his brother greeted her politely, but when the younger boy turned away, Nik remained just a second longer, long enough to flash a surreptitious vee for victory with his fingers. Then he followed his brother out.

That was all it took. Hennelyn's doubt and fear fell away, and she felt the first deep-down stir of exaltation.

Her plan had really worked!

### Letter from Arcmas – December

*Hi Hennelyn. I've been here almost three months now. I should say only three months, and something bad has already happened. I don't know if I should tell you, because I know you will worry… I've been attacked.*

# H.M. Richardson

*It was one night about two weeks ago in our barracks. A few of the other young recruits, eight of them who make up our 'team' of ten, tried to sneak up on me at night and take me outside for what they called 'disciplinary action.'*

*First of all, you know that I can't be snuck up on, since I rarely lie down to sleep. Not to mention that I wake up at the slightest sound. Maybe that's what they find so repellent about me. But they said it was because our team is lowest in the standings because of me; that I don't do as well at the drills as most others do.*

*I let them take me out of the barracks, but when I found that they meant to beat me up, I had to defend myself. I think there were really only about three who wanted to hurt me; the others were only there to back them up. The worst of it was that they called me names, like... oh never mind that. I tried not to hurt them much, and I touched no one who had not touched me. Plus, they had not brought weapons.*

*The three who did most of the punching were in the infirmary for a day or two getting patched up. And I have my own bruises. But what was I to do? And in a way, I think they are right. I don't see why I am here with the others; I thought I would be sent here to train for some kind of special duties.*

*You are probably wondering why I was confronted by only eight boys instead of nine. I think that the ninth one, a goofy character by the name of Khaydon Trenow, is trying to befriend me. In my opinion, his performance at drills is as bad as mine, because he is so clumsy at everything, but so far no one has given him any 'discipline' for it. He is the only one who eats with me in the mess hall. He started that only about a couple of weeks after I arrived. I tried to ignore him, but he's one of those people who won't take a hint.*

*I guess it's all right to have one friend here. I am still missing you and Nik a lot.*

# Chapter Eleven

On the day before Longest Night, Solit Drakhow finally awoke from his stupor. He never did remember much of what had happened during his last shift with the prisoner, though he seemed to be all right in other respects. Apparently, he had gotten an overdose of sleeping powders, and it was taking him a little while to recover. Hennelyn felt some remorse; she had not meant to harm anyone.

It didn't look as festive in the house, Hennelyn thought, as when Arcmas was there to drape streamers in the highest places around the large hall, and the day itself was not as cheerful as it could have been, even though Lisha and the other Lunians tried hard. Then came an awkward moment. Lisha noticed the new ring on her hand and asked about it.

With some dismay, Hennelyn realized that she had been wearing it openly without thinking, ever since Brinkle had given it to her.

"It's... it's... from a secret admirer," Hennelyn stammered.

"Secret to you or just to us?" Lisha wondered with an amused smile.

"Secret to me," Hennelyn lied. "The soldier that gave it to me said that it was from someone else." It sounded lame to her, but the others accepted the explanation.

"Well, well," remarked Lisha with a wink. Hennelyn deftly steered the conversation to another topic by noticing her new holiday hairstyle.

Later they exchanged small gifts, and everyone tried to ignore Arcmas's empty stool at the feast. His absence and the bunji's escape had cast a pall on the whole celebration.

It appeared that all of the soldiers had caught the mood of their commander. There was little holiday carousing among them this year. The farm families sang and partied together, visiting one another in sleighs or wagons. Nik's family celebrated in the servants' hall with Dewdra. But in the Kanow household, the usual joy was dampened.

The following day, Tai sent out four riders with a message for Siras Thraulor. Hennelyn wondered why, but she didn't ask.

December ended and January crept along, day by day. The warm spell came to an end, and snow fell many of the days. The prairie slumbered under a white blanket. The patrols were kept from their endless searches now and then by the weather, but there was nothing to indicate that the bunjis were still out there. No mischief, no sabotage. Hennelyn wondered if perhaps they had taken Brinkle and fled far away.

Jaero Lite tried to start up Hennelyn's lessons again, but she felt restless in the house and couldn't concentrate very well. Tai was patient and thorough, and his investigation of the jail-break proceeded. Sometimes, Hennelyn felt like she just wanted to flee far into the prairie and scream from suspense. Instead, she began to spend much of the cold weather in the homes of others. She visited the families of the marshal and the centenors, and practiced her trick-riding with their daughters when the weather permitted. She practiced her archery and hand-to-hand combat with Ghundrew. She set rabbit traps near the creek down below the town, and caught enough rabbits to make herself a lap blanket, with Dewdra's help. She endured many fittings of her mother's dress with Lisha.

She spied on her father's activities through Nik, asking him who had been to the soldiers' barracks for interviews while trying not to let these meetings look suspicious. Talking to him always lifted her spirits, and so far Tai's inquiries among his staff had not included the children. In fact, his investigation had been much more secretive than she had expected.

Then the patrols reported that they had spotted fresh bunji tracks. The little people were still around, it seemed.

### Letter from Arcmas – January

*Hi Hennelyn. At last my superiors have gotten the hint, I believe. I have been moved out of my barracks and into a cabin of my own. Except, strangely, Khaydon has moved along with me, so I suppose I can't say that it's only my cabin. Perhaps because everyone needs a sparring partner.*

*Khaydon and I are directly trained by Centenor Jakhron now. We no longer run drills or practice battles. Instead, the two of us spend hours mapping the terrain out here; I observe it all from the air, and Khaydon draws the maps from what I describe. He also reconnoiters some of it on foot for greater detail. He seems to have the knack for accurate mapping when he walks over the ground himself.*

*Centenor Jakhron wants me to learn to avoid arrow attacks. He lets soldiers shoot at me with big, slow, blunt-tipped arrows as I fly through a shallow valley, at first only a few, then more and more. I've had to do some fancy aerial dodging in the past week or so! The arrows can't really puncture, but I've had some spectacular bruises, and many times I've been knocked out of the sky. It's not my favorite activity, but I guess I can see the value of learning to dodge arrows.*

*And that's not all, after a while the arrows got smaller and quicker. Harder yet to dodge, and to this the centenor added body armor for me to wear. Flying in body armor! As if it wasn't difficult enough to practice these acrobatics. This is the first time in my life that my muscles have been sore merely from flying. I guess it's at least a sign that my training is specializing.*

*I also have a new hawk that I am training to take messages from me to Jakhron and vice versa. She is beautiful, almost completely white on her undersides. I've called her Whitefeather. She is getting the idea of carrying messages already.*

*Did you think of me during the Longest Night holidays? I thought of you, and everyone at home there. The soldiers celebrated out here, but it can't be the same without my family, can it? Still, Khaydon and I did the best we could with each other, since he is also without nearby family. He is so far the only one out here who sees me as just another person, like himself. He may be odd to the others, but he's becoming a good friend to me.*

January passed the snow-white mantle onto February's shoulders. Then came the day that Hennelyn had been dreading.

About three and a half weeks after the Longest Night festivities, her father interrupted her lessons, calling her up to his office. She followed him up the steps and into the small room. It was late in the afternoon, and a narrow rectangle of sun beamed through the slightly cracked-open shutters, folded itself across his desk, and pointed towards the door.

He seated her on the near side of his rough table that dominated the middle of the room. All around on spruce shelves stood his books and military accoutrements. He circled around across from her, throwing a shadow until he sat down, after which she noted with discomfort that the sunbeam shone full in her face.

Her father sat silent for a long moment, while she winked and squinted her eyes. But no matter how she tried to see, Tai's face remained unreadable, a dark silhouette. Then he spoke softly.

"Hennelyn, I have been up and down, in and out of all of the facts of this case, and of all the theories I have entertained, there seems to be only one conclusion that I can make."

He waited. She said nothing, because suddenly she could not seem to draw enough breath.

Tai went on, "What I have decided is that the bunji prisoner had help from within our own ranks. And not from within our ranks only, but even from within my own household. For a long time I could not think of any man here who could somehow gain an advantage over me by this. From there, I narrowed it down from a member of my household to my own family. And I suppose you know where that leaves us, since now there are only two to choose from – and I know for sure that it wasn't me. I also realize that if this has become obvious to me, then it must be to others, too."

Hennelyn kept her silence, but she felt his gaze press against her downcast eyes like a physical weight.

"The question that troubles me most," he continued calmly, "is not why. I think I understand why. Eventually, the most worrying question to me became what now? I've spent a lot of thought on that. And I think I have come up with a way forward. That is, a reason why my daughter is not a traitor, though it may look that way right now."

He leaned forward, and his head shadowed her face enough that she could see his expression revealed in the light reflected up from the pale wood of the desk. His face showed what his voice hadn't. There was a deep line between his brows that came not from anger, she thought, but from pain. She saw that he felt betrayed. Now she felt pain, too, sharpened by a thin blade of guilt.

"Do you want to know the reason?" he asked softly. Her eyes dampened.

"Of course, Father," she murmured.

"The reason being, my girl, that this was our plan all along! Wasn't it? We crafted the whole thing together from the start; when I saw how the bunji reacted to you, I instructed you to gain his confidence, then, when you succeeded at that, you were to pretend to aid his escape. Because that was part of our plan. Do you see? Now this is what we planned next.

"You will go out into the wilderness to find your new 'friend' and continue to work your way into their circle. Then, when the time is right, you will lead as many as you can into an ambush that we will set. I can give you, say, a week or ten days among them to find a way to do this. Maybe you will even find one or both of the Adon Mirus. You are a clever girl, and I have a great deal of confidence in you. At least, that is what I am telling everyone else. This is the ultimate Starkhon strategy, I will say. What we Starkhons cannot achieve by force, we can always get through deception."

He smiled sadly. Hennelyn's thoughts whirled.

96

"But I don't know how – what could I say to them? How would I get them to come with me into an ambush – or anywhere? Do you really think that they would follow me *back* to the Outpost?"

"You needn't bring them back. If they went in any direction, we could set the ambush in front of them. Or we could surround and capture them. As many as possible. You only need to let us know where."

"But how will you even know where I am? And how will we communicate?" she asked, an involuntary quaver in her voice.

He sighed and crossed his arms, sitting back.

"Come now, Hennelyn, you have hunted many times; you know these things. You know how to cover your trail, and you also know how to lay one. And you know all of the smoke signals. You need not fear that you will be out there alone. We will always be following at a distance. And though our dogs may not be willing to track the bunjis, I don't think that they will have any problem sniffing *you* out if need be."

She had no reply.

He added urgently, "You must see, my girl, that there is no other choice for us. Either you will be called the general's daughter who turned traitor, or you will be like young Parskhen of old, the hero maiden who warned her people of a coming attack and saved them all."

He suddenly leaned forward and placed a big warm hand over her icy one where it lay listlessly on the table. He squeezed hard.

"You must know – you *have* to know which outcome I prefer – and what you must do so that I can protect you."

This time it was his voice that sounded raspy. The unexpected tenderness prompted two of her unshed tears to spill over and lay tracks down her face, one on each cheek. They sparkled in the strong sun. On impulse, she suddenly laid her head down sideways on top of their two clasped hands.

"All right, Father," she murmured, the left edge of her lips brushing his skin, "I'll do as you say." She felt him lightly stroke her hair with his other hand.

"Thank you, my girl," he murmured. "Remember - all this is to go no further than this room! You may go now. I have much to do."

She stood up woodenly and left him, closing the door softly behind her. But once in the safety of her own room, she threw herself on her bed, crushing her face into the fur to stifle any sound that might escape.

She hardly knew how she felt. Dismayed? *Yes.* Horrified? *Yes.*

An undercurrent of relief that the suspense was finally over? *Also yes!* She had pretended to agree with her father and his 'solution.' Yet she knew with every fiber of her being that she could not - and would not - do as he asked.

Yet another emotion was struggling to emerge from the tangled strings of the others; after a moment she realized it was despair. *No! That one I can't allow! I have to be able to think this through clearly - and come up with a different solution.*

As far as Tai was concerned, the decision was made, even though he got objections as he broke the news to the Luinians at the supper table.

"But sir, how can you send her out there all alone? And in the middle of winter?" Lisha asked reproachfully.

"It would not be any different than if she were doing her 'survival week,'" Tai replied. "Many young Starkhons are sent out in the very same way before they come of age. It's our tradition. Arcmas would have done his if he hadn't had to leave us so quickly. Besides, it's warm for this time of year."

Jaero Lite offered, "Could we not report that it was I who freed the bunji? After all, I was present when he was first brought in. It was I who first questioned him. It could easily have been I who drugged the water and got him out of the tower!"

Hennelyn stared at him, touched by the sacrifice her tutor was proposing.

"It's all right, Jaero Lite. I agree with Father," she reassured him.

The next day she spent packing. Her backpack she filled with essentials, the most important being her bow and quiver of arrows. She fingered Arcmas's last gift to her, the long feather, with some regret. It was too big to take with her and would probably only get ruined anyway.

Hennelyn had of course been on hunts and slept beneath the stars before, but that had always been in the summertime. This time she would have to light fires at night to stay warm.

That evening she stood looking out of her window for a while before she climbed into bed. It had been a warm and sunny day, warm enough to melt some of the snow on the highest points of the terrain. The mountains in the west tanned from white to bronze before becoming indigo silhouettes as the sun set behind them.

Hennelyn tossed and turned with worry, not for herself, but because she hadn't had a chance to talk to Nik. There had been no chance to talk to him, to let him know that she had not compromised her convictions - she would not betray the bunjis, whatever her father said - and just maybe, she may never come back.

# Chapter Twelve

The day she was to leave dawned cloudy and cold, and fog pooled in the dells and coulees. Her father woke her just as the sun was rising. She ate a large breakfast with him before the Luinians rose and listened to his last instructions. Then he dressed for the outdoors, held her coat for her to put her arms into and loaded her up with the backpack. They stepped out together through the door. Their breath smoked in the pale light outside. He walked her through the gate and down through the silent sleeping town.

When they came down from the hills, the fog pressed intimately around them, as though to keep her departure secret from any who might be watching. It also deadened all sound except for the crunch of the snow beneath their feet. It seemed as though nothing else was alive in the landscape but for the two of them, except for the suppressed tinkle of the little spring-fed creek they crossed, running under its lid of ice. Yet Hennelyn knew that a number of soldiers were also setting out, soon to follow.

She and her father walked without speaking to the edge of the farmed lands. By that time the day had brightened considerably, and the fog was ripping up and blowing away in tatters.

Here Tai stopped. They faced each other and held each other's mittened hands. For a long moment, it seemed that he would not let her go. Then he spoke for the first time since they had stepped outdoors.

"Remember... we will never be too far away. If you get into trouble, build a signal fire."

She nodded. "I remember, Father."

He searched her face, gave a quick, encouraging smile, and turned away. She itched to give him a big hug and fill her nostrils with his manly smell one last time. But that would make him suspicious. Instead, she stood still and watched him walk away. Then she heaved a big sigh, hitched up her heavy pack, and continued on over the snow-patched prairie.

The first part of the day was easy going. She kept angling towards the river to check for bunji footprints in the snow down there, and then back up again to bare flattened grass where the snow had recently melted off. She rested often, scanning the land for any movement. She was not expecting to have to go far, for hadn't she told the bunji, Brinkle, to watch out for her? Surely they already knew that she was in their territory. But by noon, when she was out of sight of her home, she had still seen no bunjis. She nibbled on some rations from her pack and rested a bit before going on.

The day grew warm, though not warm enough to melt snow this time, and the sun made no appearance. Neither did the bunjis. *What was happening? Where were they?* The only creatures Hennelyn saw were rabbits, ravens, hawks, deer, and the everlasting chickadees, one of the few small birds that lived here the winter through, filling the cold silences with their taunting cry. She thought she saw an elk or two in the distance.

In the afternoon, she finally saw tracks near the river that were not made by animals. They looked to be those of soft bunji boots. Perhaps she was getting close.

About an hour later, she was still wandering about without success. Plodding dispiritedly through some clinging underbrush, she heard something like a purr followed by a click – the sound a raven makes. Then there was another shortly afterward. She took little notice at first; ravens are ubiquitous on the prairie.

But then the hair on the back of her neck prickled. She faltered and stopped midstep. There was a treed coulee to her left, and snow layered the ground white all around her. She felt watched. Her hand slipped under her coat unconsciously and drew out the long dagger she was carrying.

There! Only a few steps in front of her! A white shape seemed to detach itself from the snowy background and move into her view. She gave a sharp gasp. She was looking at a figure, a little shorter than herself, hooded and robed in white fur. His face was masked in white too, but he reached up and removed this, and Hennelyn found herself staring into black bunji eyes, frowning from a dark face. At last, one of them had deigned to reveal himself! This bunji was older and stockier than Brinkle, and the lower half of his face was mostly covered in a black, curly beard. Then the corner of her eye bothered her, and she peered slowly around. It was then that she saw she was surrounded.

How they had crept up on her so quietly, she didn't know. It was as though they had appeared out of thin air, and there were at least fifteen of them standing in a circle around her. It was exactly like the time that she had once been hiking among an outcropping of grey rock and had suddenly noticed one of the 'rocks' move. On closer inspection it had turned out to be some kind of grey speckled partridge. She had then discovered that there were many similar partridges all around her, completely still and identical to the rocks - in perfect camouflage. In the same way, these bunjis had surrounded her without her noticing. *Embarrassing.*

The group around her all began to unmask, and she saw that they were all male. They reached perhaps to her chin or less in height, but they all looked sturdy. Not one was as slender or as short as Brinkle. Their dark eyes regarded her suspiciously. Most of them sported neatly trimmed beards on their rounded faces, and some held long spears tipped with sharp heads of stone. One of them said something, gesturing with his spear and advancing on her. Hennelyn raised her hands defensively into the air, then seeing the dagger still in her hand, she returned it quickly to its sheath in her belt. She tried a nervous smile. Not one expression changed. They stood and stared at Hennelyn fixedly. She licked her lips.

"Is Brinkle here?" she inquired in the trade language. "I'm looking for Brinkle."

The bunji directly in front of her threw back his hood and approached, his spear leading. He stopped, holding the pointy tip of it inches from her throat.

"Woah!" Hennelyn yipped, as she skipped back a step. She kept her hands high. "I'm not here to hurt anyone. I just want to talk."

Her assailant stood still and glared at her, spear at the ready. His hair and short beard showed some silver strands, but he looked well-muscled and strong. When he spoke, she was surprised to hear how deep his voice was.

"Are you the one called Hen-lin?" he rumbled.

"Yes, Hennelyn is my name. I'm the one who helped Brinkle escape from the tower." He lowered his spear just a little, and her heartbeat slowed.

"Why do you walk out across our lands? What do you want?" His words were accented, but Hennelyn was relieved to discover that they could understand one other.

"I've come to warn you."

The bunji looked at her quizzically.

"What do you mean?"

Hennelyn took a breath.

"You know that my people are plotting to fight you, don't you?"

"Fight us? How can they? They cannot even find us!"

"You don't understand. Soon more soldiers are coming, many more. My people are determined that they should build a settlement here."

"We will stop it," the bunji warned.

"You can't," Hennelyn cautioned. "They will have their way, and sooner or later you will have to fight for your land. But I can perhaps help to delay that day. Maybe we could settle this peacefully, without any of you being killed. I've come to help you find a way and to stand between you and my people."

The bunji grunted sardonically.

"We know what the Tall Fierce People want. They have overtaken our eastern lands. We will not surrender any more. But what could you do for us? You are a child! You are not even one of them. You look like one of the Sun People who come up our western coasts from the south."

Hennelyn remembered Brinkle's name for her: Sunchild.

"You're half right about that. My mother was a Sun Woman. But I can help you, because my father is the leader of the Fierce Ones. He is like your Laero."

The point of his spear quivered menacingly.

"Then you have come to us as a spy!" he accused her tightly. "You will report to your father where you found us!"

"No! No, I really do want to help you," Hennelyn said, heart sinking. "I helped Brinkle escape, didn't I? He would have been killed if it weren't for me. Didn't he tell you?"

"Brinkle is a foolish boy. He doesn't understand people like you - a people that can lie. How would he know why you did as you did?"

It was a sharp dig, seeing that Hennelyn's father had meant exactly that when he'd sent her out – deceit. Spying. How could she prove that she wasn't here for that?

"I only did it to save his life. Please. Won't you believe me?"

The bunji's face seemed to shutter itself against her. He barked out a command in his own language. The other bunjis turned their backsand melted away, all except for four who hemmed her in on all sides with their spears. The commander turned back to her. His eyes were narrowed, and his voice hard.

"We don't believe you. Do you want to help us? Go back to the distant east - and take your people with you. Go home, little girl!" Then the remaining bunjis whirled around and trotted off in four different directions, but first one of them threw something at her feet which immediately wrapped around them. It tripped her up, and she fell down. As she looked around from there, nothing remained from their visit except the trampled snow.

Impatiently Hennelyn unwound the strange collection of twine and stones from around her ankles and tossed it aside. She'd seen these 'hobbles' before, brought in by Starkhon soldiers who had run afoul of them while chasing bunjis. She got up and broke into a run down into the coulee, taking the same path as the bunji who had spoken. But it was no use. She could hear or see nothing. She was again alone in the still, grey day.

She followed more than one set of tracks until each trail disappeared in bare grass. She could not find where any trail started up again. The bunjis had not left any bent twigs nor any other sign of their passage. Of course not. If it were that easy to find them, we would have rounded them all up a year ago!

Hennelyn's spirits plummeted. The interview had not gone well. What should she do now?

Well, first things first. It was late in the day now, time to look for a promising campsite where she could eat her evening meal. It might take a while to find a sheltered spot, and then she still needed to gather firewood and start a fire before the short winter day was over. She had dried food, a hatchet for firewood, a flint, and a steel - everything she needed.

She grew tired and hungry before a little valley suddenly opened up in the flat prairie and plunged deeply down about fifty feet, widening as it went. She slipped and slid down the slope until she reached its bottom. It turned a corner and revealed a copse of thick spruce and aspens against a short cliff of soil and stone. Beyond this point the coulee went around another sharp bend and presumably made its winding way in this fashion for a mile or more until it reached the river.

Hennelyn approached the cliff bottom, thinking it was a good place to set her back against. She found a nice little nook between two large spruces, snuggled right up tight to the natural wall. There was a small platform of rock jutting out about two feet up from the ground, which looked about the right size for her to lay on like a bed. The floor next to this was fairly level and covered with years of fallen spruce needles. Here the wind would not be able to reach her.

The sheltered space was small, but it had enough room for her to move around in and set a few things out. Nothing could approach her from the sides through the thick spruce growth, and it wasn't likely that anything would jump down from above into that small space. All she needed was a fire at the entrance to her small alcove, and she would be safe against wild animals and intruders alike. It was perfect.

First she hung her leather pack as high as she could into the spruce tree. Then, taking the hatchet, she began looking for firewood.

Soon she had a nice fire going and her small handled pot set up over it, coming to a boil. In this she placed some moose jerky to make a kind of soup — an old trail trick. She also sprinkled in some dried vegetables and herbs. For dessert, she had some dried fruit and ginger, and leaves of tea. Even a bit of honey to sweeten the tea.

Twilight faded away while she ate her soup from her tin cup with a tin spoon, and the dark of night settled in around her. A fireside was lonelier with no one else there to talk to.

She built up her fire so that it would burn a long time, and then retreated away from the extra heat to her sleeping ledge. She laid some spruce boughs down on the stone for a bit of padding, then pulled her furry bedroll out. She lay down fully dressed, boots and all, with her face towards the flames and her pack under her head for a pillow. It was not terribly comfortable, but at least she felt warm. The night made no noise that she could hear above the crackling of the fire. The blue and orange tongues of flame blurred as her eyes began to droop. Very soon she slept deeply, dreaming that she was running free through an icy night with all the other bunjis, helping to set the rainbow fires that told the mysterious midwinter tale.

Sometime later, she didn't know how long, Hennelyn woke with a start. It took a moment for her to realize that she was cold and stiff, but that was not what had jolted her awake. The hairs on the back of her neck were prickling again.

She sat up slowly and listened hard. Her fire had dwindled to a few glowing coals, and all about her was inky darkness. Just then, a long, shivery howl sounded, very close.

Wolves were on the prowl. They sounded much too close for comfort. Perhaps the lingering scent of her supper had brought them. Hennelyn knew that it was rare for wolves to attack people, but it was hard to convince herself of that when she could hear their feet rustling in the undergrowth and the sharp whiffling of their noses in the frosty air. Working as fast as her cold limbs would move, Hennelyn rose and began to rebuild the fire. Flames burst into life, licking hungrily up into the fresh fuel. The fire sent probing gold fingers out into the night beyond the spruces. Hennelyn huddled near it and let the heat bathe her.

She squinted into the edge of the darkness, suddenly skittering backwards from the fire in a fright. The shiny eyes of wolves glowed here and there, then disappearing only to wink out somewhere else. Hennelyn reached for the dagger at her waist. She had it in her hand when a particularly curious wolf approached, so close that the silvery fur of his massive head and shoulders were gilded by the flames. He fixed her with his yellow unblinking eyes and stood there, sniffing the air and letting his big tongue loll out of his mouth. He didn't growl or make any sign of aggression, but to Hennelyn's mind, he was much too close for comfort.

After a moment of frozen shock, Hennelyn inched closer to the fire, dagger first. The wolf dipped its huge head, watching. She slowly reached out a gloved hand, laying hold of the cool end of a burning ember. Carefully she fished it out of the fire. With a sudden flick of her wrist, she threw it straight at the wolf. He danced aside nimbly, untouched. He treated her to one more amber stare, turned, and vanished into the night. The last thing she saw was his bushy tail waving a saucy farewell.

Hennelyn fed her fire again, feeling safer the bigger it burned. She went back to her bed, a little rattled, thinking there would be no more sleep for her that night. But eventually she slowly tipped onto her side, and once more sank into dreams.

# Chapter Thirteen

Hennelyn woke later than she'd planned the next morning because of her lost sleep in the night. The new day was dull, and she found herself floured with a fine layer of snow when she sat up, shivering. Her neck seemed frozen into a painful bend. Although the sun was not to be seen through the smudged cottony clouds, she sensed that it was already mid-morning. The fire had burned down to nothing, and she felt like she'd never be warm again, but as she started to move around, the chills and aches of the night worked themselves out of her limbs. She ate breakfast from the provisions in her pack. She had been as careful as she could not to leave a trail, not wanting to risk making a fire during the day when the smoke might be observed.

She still felt downcast about her failure to connect with the bunjis. She had been sure that Brinkle would have vouched for her. But there was nothing else she could do but be patient and keep trying.

She packed up quickly, then shouldered her bag and walked on. She did the same as the day before: to the river, away, toward, away. Stop and eat; go on. The pack seemed heavier every hour.

The day was fairly cloudy and warm, but the breeze blew strongly. She saw a great many rabbits, as well as a pair of moose: a cow with a half-grown calf at heel, fording the ice-caked river. She gave them a wide berth.

The evening drew on. As she was detouring around a slough, a small covey of grouse exploded practically out from under her feet in the dense underbrush. With the speed of long practice, she grabbed her bow and quiver and loosed an arrow after one of them. No luck. She headed off to see if she could find the lost arrow.

She didn't find it, but she did find another good campsite; a little gravelly clearing surrounded by thick underbrush. Another night of soup made over the fire.

Day three of waking up cold and miserable again, even though she had stoked the fire several times. Her stomach felt emptier than it ever had before. The small meals she had been eating were not enough to keep up such a pace. Should she stop somewhere and lay out traps? But it could take a long time to catch prey that way.

She saw with resignation that the weather continued cloudy that morning. She had been brushing her teeth and hair every day, plaiting the unruly locks into one long braid down her back before sleeping, but she still felt rumpled and unkempt. Her toes felt a little funny - some numb, some prickly. *Better check them today for frostbite.*

She cleaned up camp and went on. At least it was interesting to scout out so much new country after having been confined these last two years so close to the Outpost. She wondered if she was taking enough care to cover her movements. Starkhons were excellent trackers, and of course she could not hope to fool the dogs unless she was taken under bunji protection. She sighed over the unlikelihood of that idea.

That day, her shoulders and legs started to ache. She would surely be sore tonight. The third day of any pack trip was always the worst physically, as she well knew.

The clouds retreated upward and thinned, and the day began to be graced with occasional sunny patches. That and the lack of wind made Hennelyn feel very warm indeed. She unfastened her heavy coat and let it gape. Before long, something like a balmy spring day invaded the winter.

Later that day, she approached the river, facing into the breeze. She headed for a spot where the water was flowing near the bank to fill her canteen. As she approached, she caught a glimpse through the tree trunks of a pair of rabbits at the edge of the river. They were only a few steps away and not yet alert to her presence. The doe was drinking, and the buck was awaiting his turn, lifting his long ears, alert for danger.

On impulse, Hennelyn unslung her bow and reached behind her shoulder for an arrow. A nice fat rabbit like that would be a tasty addition to her meager menu.

Twang! Hennelyn's arrow struck straight into the rabbit's body. It leapt into the air, unleashing its ear-splitting scream of death. The doe darted off into the bush in a panic. After that the only sound was the harsh call of ravens, broadcasting the event to the world. Hennelyn's prey thrashed a little, then lay still.

Hennelyn approached the dead animal with a twinge of regret, as always. She remembered the first deer she had brought down at the age of twelve and how she'd run away to hide her tears, not waiting to hear the congratulations of her hunting companions. But life in the wild environs of the Outpost demanded such things, and she'd learned since to take her turn providing food for the household.

It would not take long to dress the rabbit out, and this was the best place, where she could wash afterward and throw the offal into the swiftly running water. Hennelyn got out her good sharp butchering blade and set it on the ground. Then she took off her outer coat and rolled up her sleeves for the operation.

She was just about ready to start the skinning when she realized that the ravens had gone silent. A moment later, they burst out of the trees with cries of alarm. Her neck hairs all stood on end, and she torqued around to look over her shoulder. Then she saw what had approached on silent paws while she had been distracted.

It was a mountain lion, a big male. Huge, almost double her size. It was so close already! So close that she could count its whiskers. It stared at her with big yellow eyes that were a little like Arcmas' in color, only scarier. It snarled at her, and the yellow canines in its mouth were bared, as long as her middle finger.

It was strange how her thoughts shut down; she was only aware of the labored thumping of her heart and the echoes of the ravens' cries as they fled. She knelt there over her kill, frozen in fear. She knew that the best thing would be to slowly move away from the rabbit and let the lion have it, but she couldn't get her muscles to respond.

Then the mountain lion bunched its hindquarters and exploded right at her. Hennelyn screamed and threw up her arms, crashing down on her back under its crushing weight. She stabbed blindly with the knife in her hand and felt it connect somewhere. The big cat screamed in feline rage, and its fetid breath blasted her face. Then it took her left upper arm in its terrible jaws. She tried to retract her blade for another thrust, but it stuck fast, and the handle was torn from her grasp.

Then something else happened very fast. Two-legged creatures appeared and leaped about at the edges of her lion-filled vision. They were shouting. The cat released her arm to face the newcomers. It stepped off of her prone body, snarling and lashing out with its paws as it was prodded by many spears. It whirled round and round. Hennelyn pushed herself up on her unharmed elbow, and now she could see.

Those who had come to her rescue were bunjis, all dressed in tan and brown. They were jabbing and harassing the big cat, matching its movements. It suddenly jumped sideways, revealing a large dart dangling from its left haunch, and leaped out of the circle, straight over the ducked heads of two bunjis. That pair broke off and went after it.

When it was gone, the remaining bunjis turned their attention to Hennelyn. She thought perhaps she recognized a face or two from her first meeting with them, but she was not sure. Still panicked,

Hennelyn tried to get up, but her left arm gave way with the attempt. She looked down at it and was shocked by the sight. Her tunic sleeve was raggedly torn and bloodied. Overcome by nausea, she sank back down onto her back.

The bunjis moved in close, squatting down beside her. One of them gently moved the ribbons of material away to look more closely at her arm. They talked softly to one another across her prone body. For Hennelyn, it all felt unreal. Everything had happened in an eyeblink. The bunjis must have been very close to get to her so fast.

They helped her to unsteady feet, and one taller, burly bunji drew her right arm around his shoulders to support her while they walked, keeping her from stumbling over the thick undergrowth.

They seemed to walk for a long time. Before they had gotten wherever they were going, pain awakened in Hennelyn's arm, and the sunlit world greyed and brightened in rhythm with her pulse. At last she felt herself being gently laid down, but now her arm felt on fire, and it was not gentle enough. She cried out in pain and spiralled into darkness.

Later, as in a dream, she saw that a small blaze had been kindled, and her own kettle was hung over it. She was roused by someone pouring liquid into her mouth. It traced lines of fire down her throat and made her cough. Someone else was prodding at her wound, making her moan. She rolled her head over that direction to see what was happening.

She was in the bunji camp, with at least four bunji attendants from what she could see. They had cut away her tunic sleeve. One bunji was kneeling there, washing her arm with warm water. The burly one who had helped her walk was holding her, his knees under her reclining body to lift her up off the ground.

Hennelyn winced as her arm was washed. The water stung the jagged puncture wounds as if it were scalding hot. She did not know how much of the liquid she had been given, but it was having quite an effect on her. Sights and sounds were unclear, as though she were underwater.

The two bunjis spoke softly to each other as they doctored her. Of the one doing the work, she only saw the top of his dark head and a flash of teeth when he looked up and spoke. So she studied the bunji who was holding her, since he was the only one that she could see clearly.

His skin was the usual color, darker than the olive-skinned

Starkhons. His heavy, dark brown hair grew to a length that half covered his ears, as Brinkle's did. His beard and mustache were trimmed short. Both head and facial hair showed silvery strands among the black. His eyes were dark, too dark to distinguish the pupils. When he smiled reassuringly at her, these eyes crinkled pleasantly at the corners, and strong white teeth shone out below. Hennelyn was not sure, but she thought that this was the bunji who had spoken to her before. "Go home, little girl," he had said.

Her 'doctor' began to bind her arm up tightly with strips of soft hide, and that hurt. She tried to hide her discomfort, and persuaded herself that she was succeeding. That done, he bent her arm up in front of her chest and tied it into a sling which hung around her neck. By the time all was finished, Hennelyn was shivering with shock. She felt herself being wrapped up warm, but something was troubling her mind. What was it? She tried to gather up the unravelling ends of her thoughts and finally realized what it was.

"The fire..." she murmured. "Put out the fire. They will find us..." But the effort of speaking was too much for her at the moment. They gave her another draught of the fiery potion, and she felt the world slipping away from her again. She decided to let it.

She woke to the feel of a cool hand on her forehead, along with a throbbing in her arm. Slowly, she opened her eyes. With a start, she saw that she was looking straight into a close-up dusky face, smooth and free of facial hair. The light seemed to be fading on towards evening, and his black hair, framed against the fire behind him, glowed red at the ends. It was his hand that lightly rested on her skin. As he saw her wake up he withdrew it, and he took up her right hand between his own, cradling it. A smile touched Hennelyn's lips. This face she knew very well.

"Brinkle!" she breathed. He nodded and smiled back.

"You... okay?" he asked in the trade language. Hennelyn stirred and tried to sit up. Brinkle helped, and between them they got her upright. She gazed at Brinkle with pleasure.

"I tried to find you," she told him. "I told you to watch for me."

"Yes, so you did," came a deep voice nearer the fire. "And Brinkle would have run straight to you that first day, if we had let him. Foolish lad!"

Hennelyn looked in that direction, thinking that the voice was the same she'd heard before. She was right. She recognized the bunji in front of her as the one who had held a spear on her and told her to go home; he was also the same one who had held her up for the ministrations of their doctor.

He was squatting by the fire tending her own pot. It steamed away, sitting on a couple of hearthstones. In spite of his words, this bunji's glance at Brinkle was affectionate. Two other bunjis at the other side of the fire were sitting on the ground and roasting strips of meat on stripped green branches, meat from the rabbit she had killed. The firelight danced in their dark eyes. Hennelyn's alarm returned.

"The fire! I tried to tell you earlier not to light one! The patrols out there will see it and know where we are."

"There is no need to worry," the same bunji answered. "Do you think we do not know how to build a smokeless fire? And we have a watch on your patrols."

He threw a handful of something into the boiling pot, and stirred it around for a few minutes. He dipped her tin cup into it and standing up, drew nearer to offer it to her. Hennelyn pulled her hand from Brinkle's to take it.

"My name is Grogo," the bunji introduced himself. "I am Laero of this place. Brinkle is my nephew. Drink! It has healing plants in it." He indicated the mixture in her cup.

She hesitated.

"I don't think I want to sleep any more just now."

"No, this is different. No more sleeping potion," he explained. Hennelyn took the cup and tried a small sip of it. It tasted mostly of spruce needles spiced with other unknown flavors. The vapors seemed to clear her sinuses and chase the last vestiges of giddiness away. The steam wrote curlicues in the cooling air. Sitting up, she could see better what the camp they had brought her to looked like.

It was a space right next to the river, protected by a tall bank that looked as though it had been washed out by a flood sometime in the past. The only approach to the camp appeared to be a narrow neck of snowy land between the river and the bank on one end. The site had plenty of room to maneuver; a snowy space of about fifteen strides long and nine across. The bank overhung them at its top by about a foot and a half.

The bunjis had brought all of her things into the camp; she saw her bow and quiver resting nearby. Her backpack and bedroll hung high on a root protruding from the bank, out of the reach of animals.

Grogo sat down next to her on her left side, since Brinkle was on her right.

"How is the arm?" he inquired.

"It hurts," she replied.

"Yes. Fraeling over there wrapped it up. There will likely be scars. But you are lucky, the muscles are only punctured, not torn."

He gazed at her, and she studied him. This time his eyes were not hostile, though still bright and searching. Hennelyn could see in his bearing the easy confidence of a leader. She searched for words strong enough to show her gratitude to him and his followers.

"I - I thank you, sir, for helping me. I didn't think that you would have bothered."

"We could not have stood by and watched a *swoll* kill a child. We have been near you all this time, very near, though you did not see us."

"Really? Well, thank you again. I should have known that you could easily see what we Starkhons were up to. I don't know if you'll believe me... but even though I *was* sent out as a spy, it isn't my intent to obey those orders."

"Little girl — I mean Hen-lin — what, then, do you want?" Grogo demanded. Hennelyn considered how to answer. It would be important to choose her words carefully, but her mind felt fuzzy and unclear.

"I've told you why I am here. I want to help you avoid a war with us. Starkhons are powerful and clever fighters. You can't win, if it should come to that."

"Bunjis do not kill any thinking peoples if we can possibly avoid it. But we will defend ourselves and these lands if we must. There are more of us, some who will come out of the west to our help if we call them, and all of us together could drive you away. We will no longer live as slaves or fugitives in our own country, like those of us who have been conquered east of here."

"That's what might have to happen in the end, I suppose," Hennelyn agreed. "But I wasn't thinking of that. I only wanted to stop our part of it — Father's part of it."

Grogo was bewildered. "But why? Why do you want to help my people instead of your own?" he asked.

Hennelyn stared into the writhing heart of the fire. At last, she said quietly, "Because when it comes to stealing the homes and lives of others... my people are doing wrong."

She could see that Grogo was surprised. He shook his head.

"You seem to be the only one of your nation who understands that, perhaps because you are also descended from the gentle Sun

People. But you will not be able to change all the rest of your folk, probably not even your father. Brinkle and Sartle have told us of the cruelty of his men, and of your father's threats.

"I don't want you to think, child, that I am not grateful to you for saving Brinkle. He is my sister's only child, and I love him as though he were my own son. It was with great joy that we welcomed him back among us. But I think that this is the most you can do for us. It is much better that you should go back to your family. Adon will help us, as He always has. Let us build your signal fire tomorrow so that the others will take you back home."

"No, I won't," Hennelyn asserted stubbornly. "I will follow you instead!"

Grogo nodded complacently.

"We shall see," he said. Brinkle had been following the conversation as well as he could, and now he said something to his uncle which brought a sharp retort. The older bunji spoke to the others near the fire, and they jumped up to gather some of the cooked food to bring to Hennelyn.

Twilight was upon the land now, and a few stars began to glimmer in the evening sky above. Hennelyn ate and drank as well as she could with one hand and with Brinkle helping her. She listened to their soft-sounding language as they talked together and wondered if she should tell them the rest of her problems. *Would they even care?*

When Grogo was finished eating, he brought over some more of the strong drink she'd had before. "It will dull the pain, and help you to sleep," he explained.

She sipped some of it. It was then that she decided to go ahead and play her last card.

"Laero Grogo, listen to me!" she insisted. "You can't send me home."

"And why not? You need the care of your family."

"Because - when I helped Brinkle escape, I betrayed my father. And to betray him is to betray my people. I am a traitor."

Grogo's look softened.

"Yes. But you will be forgiven. You are only a child."

"You don't understand. My orders were not to return unless I brought one or more of you back with me. It's the only way I can be forgiven of treason in the eyes of the Starkhons. Do you see now? You will be sending me back to a trial - and perhaps death."

Grogo stared at her in silence. But Brinkle understood her last words just fine, for he leaped to his feet and looked down at her with wide eyes.

"I don't believe you," Grogo murmured at last. "No father would not welcome back his lost daughter, no matter what she'd done. No people except the ancient Mollins kill their own children."

"I didn't say that it was up to my father. It's the way we live, whether Father agrees with it or not," Hennelyn replied wearily. She suddenly felt as though all of her energy had leaked out with her words. "I can't talk about it anymore today. Just don't alert the patrols tomorrow, okay? Please?"

Her eyelids began to droop.

Brinkle addressed his uncle again, urgently, and they exchanged a couple of sentences. Hennelyn tried to stand, but dizziness overcame her, and she sank back down instead. The bunjis broke off their conversation. They gently helped her lie down and tucked the pelts around her. Then they retreated to the other side of the fire. One of them fed the blaze a little bit. Then all of them stayed seated on the ground there, talking softly but intently in their own tongue to one another. Their quiet voices washed over her until she drifted off to sleep, wondering what they would decide to do about her.

·

# Chapter Fourteen

## Letter from Arcmas – February

*Hi Hennelyn. I am still writing these letters, although there has been no one travelling west all these months to deliver them to you, as far as I know. There should be someone going there soon; surely you all need new supplies by now.*

*I wish I had you here to talk to. Something terrible has happened. Khaydon is hurt. For almost a month, everything went well, just the two of us training with Jakhron, and staying at our own place at the edge of the grounds, eating and sleeping apart from the others. Then yesterday Jakhron and I were called into the Ambassador's house in town for a briefing. We rode our horses in. When we returned, Jakhron left me to head for the officers' quarters, and I went on alone from the stables to the cabin I shared with Khaydon.*

*When I got there, there was a fight going on! This time it was Khaydon being attacked by a group of other recruits. I didn't even think; I just waded in. I was so angry, I couldn't restrain myself. Most of them were down by the time I finished. But it was too late to protect Khaydon. He has some kind of internal injuries, and they don't know if he will pull through. The worst of it is that they say one of the other boys can't wake because of how I hurt him. I hope he wakes up soon.*

*Why did this happen? I don't understand it. Why do we fight one another in this place instead of the enemy? And who is our enemy anyway? These bunjis? They have not declared war on us as far as I know. There doesn't seem to be much reason at all for this training, or for this military envy, if that's what it is that causes the fights. If I didn't know that it would dishonor Father, I would just fly home.*

*I am done with this. They won't be able to get one more day of this senseless training out of me, no matter what they do. I don't want to hurt anyone else again. Ever.*

Hennelyn slept late into the morning again. She opened her eyes to see a two-sided deerskin tent set up over her. Turning her head, she saw that some light snow was falling. The bunjis were up and about. Grogo and Brinkle were still there, but different bunjis had replaced their companions during the night. A stranger was brewing yet more tea over the fire. There was another moving beyond him, taking breakfast things out of a small sack. After a time, he approached the fire and began

# The Prisoner and the Traitor

to cook something suspiciously like porridge in a bigger pot that wasn't Hennelyn's. He looked old enough for a beard, but his facial hair was trimmed very short so that it drew a two-inch thick line across the bottom of his chin, and up in front of his ears.

Hennelyn tried unsteadily to sit up, and that brought Grogo and Brinkle quickly to her side. Grogo looked into her face and lifted a hand to her forehead.

"Do you feel better now?" he asked with concern.

"Yes," Hennelyn answered, but she still felt a little shaky, and her arm seemed, if anything, worse. It throbbed, hot and swollen.

"I will send for Fraeling to change the bandages," Grogo told her. "We must be careful with a swoll bite like this. They are notorious for causing the 'wound fever.'."

He motioned to the other bunji and spoke. Immediately the other left the camp. Brinkle saw her struggling to sit up and helped her.

"What is this 'swall' you are talking about?" she asked Grogo.

"I ask your pardon. I know the trade language well, but I do not know the animal names. Swoll is our name for this big animal that bit you yesterday. What do you call it?"

"Oh. The mountain lion. We call those mountain lions."

"Mountain lie-ons," he repeated. "Odd name for a beast that roams both mountain and prairie."

"Yes, they look like the lions back in our homeland, but different enough to need a different name."

Then Hennelyn asked the question burning in her mind: "So what have you decided about me? Are you giving me up today?"

A glance passed between Grogo and Brinkle.

"We have consulted Adon," he answered, "and we have decided that you should stay with us – for the time being. We have no desire to put you in danger with your own people. We will not move camp today yet, but I think we must tomorrow."

Brinkle smiled at her obvious relief.

"Adon," she repeated quizzically. There was so much she wanted to ask about this Adon! Later.

She was amazed at her own weakness when she tried to move around. She had not realized how much an animal bite would affect a strong young girl like herself. Her arm throbbed, and it seemed to spread an extra tenderness throughout her whole body. Fraeling returned to treat her wound, unwrapping, washing, and bandaging it again. The arm protested painfully at his touch. But she made it through the operation

117

with little more than some wincing.

Fraeling smiled at her when he was done. Today she could see him clearly. He also had a short-cut beard, oddly hazel eyes, and perfect teeth.

"You are a brave child," he told her in his heavily-accented trade speech.

"Thanks," she answered wryly, a bit embarrassed. He helped her draw the blankets around her shoulders before he gathered everything up and left. Grogo then approached with two cups. Hennelyn's nose told her it was the spruce-tasting stuff she'd had before.

"Your medicine."

She took it, and he handed the other cup to Brinkle. "For you, boy."

Hennelyn asked curiously, "Why are you always calling Brinkle a 'boy' or a 'lad'? Isn't he nineteen years old?"

"Do you see any beard on his chin yet?" Grogo chuckled. Brinkle seemed to understand this. He shot his uncle a reproachful look.

Grogo went on, "Bunji lads are not grown until they see twenty-four summers, and their beards begin to grow. Twenty-four, twice the number of a Laero's counselors. Brinkle only just escaped being sent away west with our wives and children a year ago. He begged me to let him stay with the men. I regretted saying yes when he was taken by your soldiers. But Adon heard our prayers for him... and sent us you."

Hennelyn started. *That name again!*

"That's what I wanted to ask you before! Who is this – this Adon you are always talking about?"

"Do you not know Adon? Have you no name for Him among yourselves? Who do your people say has created everything we see around us? Who has created all the thinking peoples?"

She stared at him, confused.

"We don't think anyone made everything. We just think it's here. It has always been here. And people are just animals who are smarter than the others."

Grogo shook his head sadly. He tried again.

"What is the most beautiful thing someone made that you can remember?" he asked unexpectedly.

Hennelyn thought.

"Well... when we still lived in Flaethe, many years ago – I think I was perhaps six years old – my mother and our maid Dewdra sewed a gown together, for Mother. It was a beautiful green, but even better

118

were the leaves and flowers that Mother embroidered on the bodice. All different shades of red and pink - I never saw anything prettier on a dress than those flowers."

"And you looked at that and admired her skill? You thought it was worth your praise?"

"Yes, of course."

"And yet you can look at the real flowers and leaves here in our world in the summer, and not know that they have been carefully and thoughtfully made? For they are more complicated than your mother's work. Much more so, because they are alive!"

"Yes, they are alive... but because they came from life. The trees were seeds that came from their parent trees," Hennelyn pointed out.

"But where did that parent tree come from? And before it? And yet before that? Where did that first spark of life come from, if not from Someone who could give life? And what about the peoples of the world? Where did we receive life, and thought, and speech, and... and music, and hands that create beautiful things, if these were not gifts from Someone else who thought, spoke, and made music and things? You can see that the animals do not have the same gifts as people do."

"I... I never thought of 'firsts.' I've only thought of 'always,' all of this has always been here." She saw that Brinkle was avidly listening, with a frown of concentration.

Grogo added, "But you see all around that that is not how the world works. You see that everything has a beginning and an end, beginning and end, over and over again with every creature. If so, one thinks that with all these beginnings and endings, there must also be a Beginning and End, for everything. It is like... I am sorry. It is hard to be clear in this language." He shook his head in dismay, defeated by lack of the proper words.

After a pause, Hennelyn said carefully, "So you think this Adon was the one who began all things?"

"Yes, just as you say."

All sorts of questions filled Hennelyn's head, but just then the other bunji approached with their bowls of hot breakfast, handing one to each of them. Ribbons of steam curled out from the hot food. Grogo took his bowl and stirred his cereal around to cool it a bit.

"We call this 'flotha.'" Grogo told her. "And you?"

"Porridge."

But this *flotha* was much better than the Starkhon porridge they made at home. It had dried berries and bits of apple in it, and, she thought, nuts and spices. Very tasty. She watched as Brinkle took a hasty bite and had to juggle the scalding stuff around his mouth until it was cool enough to chew. His antics made Hennelyn laugh. He looked pleased to have amused her.

Now that the young bunji was free under the sky and not imprisoned in a dark tower, his smiles came easy and often. There was no longer any sign of bruising on his face, and his dark eyes sparkled with health and cheerfulness. Seeing this, Hennelyn's last doubts about saving him fled away. For the first time, she felt completely glad about what she had done, betrayal and all. If only her father could be here to see this.

After breakfast, the other three bunjis went off on an errand, but Brinkle stayed with her all morning and past a quick bite at lunchtime. He even helped her brush out and pull back her thick hair when he saw her trying to tackle this daily ritual with only one hand.

Later that afternoon, she began to feel feverish and tired. Fortunately, Grogo had left some of the fiery liquor behind, and Brinkle gave her a couple of mouthfuls of that. As usual, it sent her quickly off to sleep. About an hour later when the others returned, it was to find Hennelyn and Brinkle both napping, she with her head on his lap, and he slumped back against the earthen wall, his arms crossed on his chest. The others smiled to see it.

Hennelyn was dreaming. In her dream, she saw herself pillowed on Brinkle's legs and noticed the other bunjis returning. She heard their soft voices as they spoke - and she could understand their words!

"How is she?" one of them asked Brinkle.

"She has a low fever," he answered, "But I don't think it will come to much. It is difficult to hold off all the poison of a swoll bite." He looked at his uncle as he continued, "It's not good enough to try to tend her out of doors like this. She should be brought to our camp west of here, in the Circle Valley. There she would be out of the weather, with a real roof over her head."

"Well, Brinkle, maybe you're right," Grogo admitted.

"I am glad that she is going to stay with us."

"For now," Grogo sighed. "But I can't help thinking that she would be better off with her own family."

"But uncle! You heard what she said. Trial and perhaps death, that's all that waits for her there."

"I am not totally convinced of that. Surely they will have pity on one of their own, young as she is."

A shadow passed over Brinkle's face. "Perhaps. But then you haven't been among them as I have. There is no mercy in them; their eyes are as black and cold as winter water."

Hennelyn saw her own sleeping form stir, and Brinkle lowered his voice. "She risked her life to save mine, now I would do the same for her."

"Yes, Brinkle, I know that you would. But I am Laero, and I must think of all of us. I am wondering how many more days the soldiers out there will wait before they start actively searching for her rather than waiting for a signal."

"I don't mean this disrespectfully, uncle, but - so what? They have always been searching, but they cannot find us."

"They found you," Grogo reminded him.

"Adon meant it to happen. It was there that this child and I met. Now we have help unlooked for," the youngster pointed out with devastating logic. The other two bunjis laughed.

"Don't you know yet, Laero, that you cannot win a war of words with your sister's son?" one of them chided.

"Yes, I do know it!" Grogo retorted. "He's been twisting me into loops from the time that he could speak his first words!" He sighed heavily.

As she slept their voices grew louder, and Hennelyn suddenly woke, lifting her lids dazedly. She looked around and saw the bunjis around her, talking, just as she had seen them in the dream. Unfortunately she could no longer understand their words as she could while dreaming. She sat up slowly, feeling a little self-conscious and disoriented. The dream had seemed so real!

"Have I been asleep long?" she yawned. "What time is it?"

"Suppertime!" cried one of the others.

"So it is," Grogo agreed. "We will now eat. We will sleep here tonight. And tomorrow, we will move you to one of our houses to recover completely, if all goes well."

Hennelyn was thrilled. *They were not sending her away! Or at least not yet.*

Just then the evening sun broke free of the clouds in the west, a scintillating orange ball hovering over the mountain peaks. Everything glowed vividly in the amber light.

One of the bunjis cooked a fine tasty stew, which the five of them ate together. It was very warming, countering the evening cold as she ate it.

"Now it is time that you should lie down and sleep again," Grogo told her kindly. "Tomorrow we will have work to do. How is the arm?"

"It still hurts some," Hennelyn hedged. Brinkle was not fooled.

"It hurts much," he clarified to his uncle. So they doctored Hennelyn with more tea and a drink from the flask, and then carefully arranged her for sleep. She lay down and savored the languor that always came after a swallow of the sleep-stuff.

For a while, she gazed out at the others as they started to settle down themselves. Then, to her surprise, the bunji who had not cooked took a small wooden pipe out from his clothing and began to blow a sweet-sounding little tune on it, his face tilted up to the darkening sky. It was a pleasing melody, and far away the coyotes seemed to howl along. The other bunjis took up the strain and sang softly along in their own tongue. She did not know what it meant, but it was peaceful and reassuring. Presently she fell asleep, with the music echoing in her ears.

The next day dawned sunny, and the bunjis would have left the place for the Circle Valley, as they called it, but Hennelyn's fever was worse. The decision was made not to move her. Instead, they let down the remaining two sides of her little tent, and Fraeling came to stay in it with her to do all the requisite nursing. By the time her fever broke, a day and a night had passed. Without her being able to mark it, the anniversary of a whole week of her mission had gone by, and the calendar clicked over to enter the month of March.

# Chapter Fifteen

Flap, flap, *flap!*

And again, flap, flap!

The noise was repetitive and irritating enough to wake her. Hennelyn looked around to see that she was enclosed by dull brown walls which were heaving in an inexplicable fashion while snow crystals sometimes dashed against the crown of her head and her brow. After a moment, she realized foggily that the day outside must be windy, blowing snow around. She was so wrapped up in blankets and furs that only her head was open to the cold air. She seemed to be alone - until the moment someone entered the small tent and fastened down the door to stop the flapping. As the figure worked at this with his back to her, she drifted once more into unconsciousness.

When she next woke, it appeared to be the morning of a new day. The familiar smell of the bunji's porridge was in the air, and the tent walls had turned golden.

Hennelyn's mouth felt like a tomb filled with smelly dead things. Her hair was still braided, but it itched and desperately needed a wash. She was so hungry that she imagined she could feel the walls of her stomach clinging together. Every movement released a rank whiff of her own stale sweat. Since she was so seldom ill, she was already impatient with it.

She groggily struggled to sit up. At that moment, Fraeling entered the tent with a bowl of steaming porridge, his breath smoking up in front of his face.

She rasped out the first burning question on her mind, "How long have I been sick?" Fraeling held up two fingers.

"Only one night. And one day."

"Where are my clothes?" was the next important question as she realized she was only clad in her spare long underwear.

"We washed them. They are drying."

He flipped open the door for her to see. There they were – her tunic, breeches and the original pair of long underwear strung over the fire. Apparently Fraeling had switched out her clothing as she slept.

Perhaps she was turning red at the thought, for he assured her, "Do not worry. I am a doctor." *As if that helps!* she thought in embarrassment.

After breakfast Hennelyn steeled herself one more time for the changing of her bandage. It hurt much less than before. By the pleased expression on Fraeling's face, it seemed that she was healing up nicely. To her it still looked awful; the puncture edges were an angry red, and the whole of her upper arm glowed yellow and purple. But the wound was now dry instead of oozing like before. When she cautiously touched her fingers to the place, it felt hot to her fingers.

Brinkle and Grogo entered the clearing as she was eating and came straight to her tent. They seemed very pleased to see her sitting up.

"Feel better now?" Brinkle asked. He sat down cross-legged at her side. Fraeling climbed out to make space for Grogo to enter.

"Yes, I do, Brinkle. Thanks. *Many* thanks!" It was a small word for the huge gratitude that she really felt. Only a few days before, she and the bunjis had been complete strangers, but since then they had all looked after her like one of their own, especially Fraeling.

"It is very good to see you better," Grogo said warmly. "Adon heard our prayers. And your people have not tried to seek you out yet, which is also good. We thought we might have to carry you away while you were ill."

"Are we going to the Circle Valley today then?" Hennelyn wondered. Grogo's black brows shot up in surprise.

"How do you know where we mean to go?" he blurted out.

She shrugged. "I don't know..." It seemed silly to say that she had dreamed about it.

"Well, we are planning to go there. But you would not make it today. Tomorrow, or even the day after, when you have some more strength. Today... rest and eat!"

That was what she did. Hennelyn felt much better after washing herself off a bit with a wet rag, brushing her teeth and hair, and getting a little help to rebraid the latter. It really needed a wash but that would have to wait. Fraeling thought it was too cold to get her head wet in the open air ("Even though this is an unusually warm winter!" he exclaimed.) Later she was able to dress herself in her clothes, warm from the fire, and get Fraeling's help to ease her arm back into the sling. The day continued sunny, with only a few downy clouds passing over, but it did not get melting warm.

Still, Hennelyn felt cozy sitting outside near the fire wrapped in her fur blanket, not having to move except for the times, as most people do, she needed a little privacy away from other eyes. Brinkle took the opportunity to practice some new words and phrases in the trade language with her. Tuppin – she thought it was him – cooked the meals, and Grogo was repacking her backpack. Fraeling had gone out of the site, probably to catch up on lost sleep.

She liked to hear them talk to one another in their own tongue. It seemed to be a language of gentleness and affection. The scene struck Hennelyn as strangely domestic, as though she were camping out with family. Evening drew on; the light was westering and one bright star sparkled over the half-frozen river in the purpling sky.

Then, suddenly, a swift-footed bunji arrived out of the twilight. He ran into the campsite and spoke rapidly and breathlessly to Grogo. He listened to instruction and nodded. All of the bunjis there stood up; they began to gather things, moving them out of the camp. Some returned carrying white rabbit furs and spread them over the roof of Hennelyn's tent. They also put up a large makeshift shelter high over the fire and covered that with white fur as well.

After this flurry of activity, the four bunjis who had spent the day with Hennelyn all sat back down again under the fire-shelter. She was bursting with curiosity.

"What is it? Are the patrols getting near?" she wanted to know.

"No," answered Grogo. "The Aesthe has been seen again, flying in the sky around your home. It seems he has returned. And many soldiers with him."

"Flying…? But… what's an 'ay-es-thee'?"

She was shocked speechless by his answer.

"It means 'Sky-master', or 'Lord of the sky'. The one who always lived in your house with you is here. He was gone some months, but now he is back."

He glanced upwards at the underside of their shelter. "Now we shall have to beware of being seen from the air, too. We cannot keep a watch on *him*."

Hennelyn put her free hand to her mouth to still a sudden trembling in her lips. After a silence in which her heart seemed to soar like an arrow and then dive like a spent one, she noticed that all of the others were watching her.

"Arcmas is back!" she gasped.

Grogo nodded. "Now we will *need* to get to the Circle Valley, Hen-lin, though you are not at your full strength. It is the only place where we can hide from the Aesthe's sharp eyes. No more camping in the open. We will move at dusk tomorrow."

But the bunji messenger had not yet finished his report, interrupting Grogo and babbling a few more sentences in their language. All of the other bunji faces turned grave.

"What? What else has happened?!" cried Hennelyn.

"Our Adon Mirus are missing," Grogo told her worriedly, "since last night."

"But where to? Not dead, surely?"

"No, we believe captured. By your Aesthe. The bunji who found their hideout empty also found a large feather in the room, and signs of a struggle. Why did anyone even go there?" Grogo questioned angrily, speaking more to himself than anyone else. "My instructions were for everyone to stay far away from them!"

"We've all been worried about them, Laero Grogo," soothed Fraeling. "Sooner or later someone would have had to bring them food anyway. How could we know that Grindle would be seen from the air?"

Hennelyn said with dull certainty, "Of course it was Arcmas. It was what they spent all these months training him for."

He had completely succeeded where she had refused to. Now all that she had done was for nothing; her efforts on Brinkle's behalf, her successes, her betrayals... everything! The ruin of all her plans made her feel dizzy and uneasy. A hard knot of anger towards Arcmas twisted in her belly - the first time she had ever felt such a thing in connection with him.

There was a long silence in which everyone silently stared blankly before them until Hennelyn broke it.

"I am going back home," she announced, suddenly sitting up tall. All heads swivelled towards her.

"What?" Grogo bellowed.

"No, you can't!" cried Brinkle.

"He's right," continued Grogo. "What about your treason? What about the trial? And you have not yet recovered completely."

Hennelyn's brows drew together. She hoped they could not see how she was quaking inside. But she knew what she had to do.

"It doesn't matter anymore. They won't care about me now, not for a long time. They have what they want." She felt that it was a gamble to go back; she didn't really know if her father could still protect her. But she knew he would try - hard.

Hennelyn matched eyes with every one of these bunjis, realizing that they had become friends.

"Besides, who will get them out of there if it isn't me?" she asked, a question to which no one had an answer. She had spoken almost flippantly, though inside she quailed from such a huge undertaking. Yet I have to attempt it. Somehow.

Later that night, as she was trying to sleep, her mind kept revolving around this new problem - and Arcmas. *I guess I should have known that this would happen. But though I know my brother has to be involved, I can't even imagine him doing this. What could have happened to him out there these six months at the training base? How did they convince him to do this?* She had no answers to her questions. Finally, worn out by worry and sick at heart, she fell into a troubled sleep.

She had no answers to her questions. Finally, worn out by worry and sick at heart, she fell into a troubled sleep.

# Chapter Sixteen

### Letter from Arcmas – February

*Hi Hennelyn. You may not have expected any more letters from me. I actually didn't think I could ever move again, even to write. I have been grounded, in the literal sense, forbidden to leave my cabin these four days since I have refused to obey any orders. But today, something happened —*

Arcmas hesitated, pen poised. Then, slowly, he lowered his quill to the paper:

*Early this morning, Centenor Jakhron told me that a priest of the emperor, a tolkhron, waited for me in Ambassador Siras Thraulor's house. Not the High Tolkhron, but a tolkhron nevertheless, sent by Tol Lorsumn himself. Of course I went with Jakhron to meet him. You know we as a family haven't really ever known priests nearby before — they are treated much more importantly than any officer. When we arrived at the ambassador's house, I entered alone, but Siras Thraulor escorted me into his upper hall, into the exalted priest's presence —*

The pen dropped from Arcmas's hand. He was certain he could not bring himself to write of these things, not even if Hennelyn were able to read about it. He vividly remembered the scene…

Siras had instructed him sternly, "Most importantly, you must bow down on one knee when we enter the tolkhron's presence. He is here on command of the emperor himself!"

Arcmas understood that very well. Emperor Tol Lorsumn was the unseen guest of every celebration, the absent High General of every conquest, the unbreakable clincher of every vow. He was more than just a king. He was said to possess many mysterious and omniscient powers. He demanded not only obedience and reverence from his people but something close to worship. This priest who had come here was the representative of that divine authority.

Siras was adding, "Do not rise without his permission. And you *must* obey his every whim. If you address him, be sure to use his title of

Tolkhron Trokh more than once, just Tolkhron in between."

Soon they approached the waiting door, closed with a guard standing in front of it, who saluted smartly and stood aside for them. Siras knocked politely, and Arcmas heard the voice of the priest bidding them enter. It sounded low and husky, as though the speaker had a case of laryngitis. The room was dark as they entered, and a robed figure bent over a table with its back to them. All the heavy curtains were closed. The guard pulled the door shut behind them. Siras sank to one knee and Arcmas followed suit.

With a rustle of robes, the priest turned around. Arcmas was afraid to look at him and continued to contemplate the intricate design of the fine rug beneath his long foot.

"Ah, Ambassador. I am pleased that you are here - and your guest, also. You may rise." Siras unbent himself and nudged Arcmas to stand up too.

His first sight of a priest startled Arcmas. For one thing, he had not expected the man to be wearing a helmet. There was light enough to see that it was like a soldier's helmet, except that this one had a piece built into it which covered the priest's eyes and nose. It glowed dimly bronze. Below it, he wore a grey-white beard and moustache of medium length.

"I sincerely hope that we have not made you wait, Tolkhron Trokh," ventured Siras in a humble tone that Arcmas had never heard him use before. The priest seemed not to hear. His hidden eyes were fixed on Arcmas, who stifled a cold shiver under the intense gaze.

The robe the man was wearing seemed to be of a deep royal blue, and so was the uniform he had on, a uniform much looser than a soldier's, composed of many cross-windings of material. The lining of the robe shimmered in the dim light, a rich bronze just like the helmet.

"So this is he, is it... young Solit Arcmas, ward of Emperor Tol Lorsumn?"

Siras started to answer, but the priest cut him short: "Never mind, Siras, of course I can see that it is," he added. Arcmas was amazed at the priest's arrogance towards the ambassador.

The tolkhron moved a little closer to the two of them, and Arcmas saw that there was something on the table behind him which emitted a blue glow. Arcmas's eyes flitted from the odd blue light to the priest's strange appearance.

*Why the eye mask? What was the man hiding? Or did all priests similarly cover their faces?*

The priest came very close, looking down on Arcmas from a height about the same as Siras's.

"So," he murmured, "You are the soldier who has stopped taking orders."

Arcmas dropped his eyes, not sure if he was meant to give an answer. Without waiting for one, the priest went on, "Siras, you may go now. Wait downstairs until I am pleased to send for you. I want some words with this recruit alone."

Siras's thin lips twitched, but all he said was, "As you wish, Tolkhron." He bowed his head just a little as he turned away. Then he was through the door and gone, letting the guard shut it behind him.

As he went, the priest moved to both of the windows and swished open the curtains. Cold winter light flooded in and fell full on Arcmas, dazzling his eyes.

"We need not speak in the dark," the priest husked, "since I no longer need to consult the Mirror of Seeing. It is sometimes easier to use it in dim light; the miles that separate me from the emperor make his image weak in daylight."

Arcmas couldn't help another nervous glance at the magical round piece of glass lying on the table, rimmed with strange bulbous figures molded from a metal which looked like gold.

Trokh stepped nearer, and Arcmas fought the urge to lean away.

"Tell me, boy, if you know, what is to be done with a solit who will not follow orders?"

*What can I say?* Arcmas thought. *That I have spent half my life in the Luinian city of Flaethe, where there were no soldiers? That my Luinian tutor has fitted me better to be a scholar than a soldier? That though I've been taught to fight well, it was just a game? That I am too young - not ready to learn to hurt or kill?*

Even if Arcmas could have articulated all these jumbled thoughts, these were not things one told a priest, a man who stood in for the great Emperor Tol Lorsumn himself.

Head bowed, Arcmas stammered, "I do want to follow orders, sir – Tolkhron Trokh – but I have not heard them yet! I mean, Tolkhron, that I have not been told what I am here for. I will fight, if it is needed. But where - ?" He broke off, afraid that he was babbling.

"Ask your question, Solit Arcmas," the priest invited.

"Where is the enemy? Are these bunjis really our enemies?"

The man's answer was firm.

"Yes. They are our enemies. Anyone who does not revere the emperor is our enemy. Anyone who gets in his way. Anyone who does not think as the emperor wishes him to think is our enemy."

"Even if the one who thinks differently... is Starkhon, sir?"

"*Especially* then. That would make him a Dissenter. And everyone knows what to do with dissenters."

He quoted from the 100 Rules and Principles: "'First, dissenters are ridiculed, then isolated, then blamed – for whatever crimes we wish to hold them responsible for – and then it is permissible for any one of us to steal their property, their homes, and yes, even their lives.' The formula has worked for centuries. Every Starkhon child learns this at their parents' knees. Did you not learn it?" His voice deepened ominously. "Or are *you* a dissenter, Arcmas?"

The youngster's heart and breath both stuttered. He gave the only possible answer.

"No I am not, Tolkhron."

"Good. I rejoice to hear it. It will be better for your father and your sister if you are not."

*There it was.* This bald threat, though not completely unexpected, still filled Arcmas with dismay. So this was how it felt to know that the fate of his family depended on him.

Trokh went on, "You will get your orders. Tomorrow. And you will obey them." Then he asked something that *was* unexpected. "May I see your hand?"

Arcmas hesitatingly reached out the closest one, his right. The priest grasped it strongly, and turned it this way and that. Then he ran his thumb firmly over the edge of Arcmas's middle claw. He dropped Arcmas's hand suddenly, and the youth stifled a gasp when he saw red blood welling from a small cut. But Trokh seemed more pleased than anything else.

"Yes! Excellent," he exulted, to Arcmas's astonishment. "Let me see your wingspan," he then demanded.

Arcmas recalled Siras's words: *obey his every whim.* He slowly unfurled his wings and stretched them out. Spread, they seemed to fill the small room. The tolkhron faltered back a couple of paces. Arcmas understood; he had had the same effect on many others. He knew that opening his wings seemed to triple his size. The rich colors of his plumage glowed in the light, rainbow glints within the darkest feathers.

Trokh gazed at him frankly, until Arcmas's face grew hot with embarrassment. Unconsciously he closed his wings, as though wilting under the priest's scrutiny.

"Very good!" Trokh exclaimed. "You do not even need

weapons. You *are* a weapon. And one that will serve us well. You must excuse my staring; when I last saw you, you were nothing but a downy little nestling – and I gave you into the care of your adopted family, hoping that one day we would make good use of you. You have grown much since then."

"But... you brought me to them? I thought it was the emperor himself who gave me..." Arcmas trailed off in confusion.

"A figure of speech only," Trokh dismissed. "It was I who sent you along with Ambassador Siras Thraulor, thirteen years ago. But actually you are a true ward of the emperor, having no family of your own."

For the first time, Arcmas looked straight into the other man's face, searching to see if he spoke truth. He was struck by how unpleasant an impression the man's looks made on him.

The tolkhron's clothes were rich, and the metal of his masking helmet appeared to be real bronze. But his skin looked pale and unhealthy for a Starkhon. His mouth was wide and his lips thick, like two fat worms lying side by side, surrounded by the coarse facial hair. His eyes were mostly shielded behind the mask, which was molded above them into eye-brow humps, but Arcmas got an impression that these orbs were not the usual brown. They seemed to gleam from the shadow of the mask in a strange way, as though they were as pale as his skin.

Cold fingers of fear skittered up Arcmas's back at the same time that his heart sank almost into his gut. There was no way to discern anything from a shuttered face like this. And yet – if this priest had known Arcmas back then, then perhaps *he* had the information that Arcmas so desperately desired.

Trokh seemed amused by his probing gaze.

"Now you are looking at me like a man. Like a soldier. Was there something else you wished to ask, Solit Arcmas? I will allow one more question."

"Yes, Tolkhron. Thank you. You say I had no family of my own. Then where... where did you find me? Where am I from?"

Arcmas did not like the way the priest's thick lips writhed into a humorless smile. Trokh stepped uncomfortably close, sidling in just behind the youngster's right shoulder, talking into his ear on that side.

He rasped quietly, "You want to know just who and what you are, isn't that right, Solit?"

Arcmas couldn't reply. He suddenly found it hard to breathe

and impossible to speak. He waited in insupportable suspense. The priest's voice sank to a hiss.

"Know this then, Arcmas... *I* created you. Using powers that you cannot imagine, with the sanction and aid of the emperor, I took an abandoned infant and fashioned him into what I wanted. You are Ours; Our vision and Our handiwork. Our creation."

Arcmas stood unmoving, as though his airy bones had just solidified into stone. All the years of longing... of wondering... to be told he was – no one? *An abandoned infant.*

The whisper of the priest's clothes as he drew away seemed unnaturally magnified. But louder still in Arcmas's ears was the thudding of his own heart. He felt about to faint, realizing in that moment it was because he had ceased to breathe. He pulled in a shaky gasp of air and the vertigo slowly receded.

He fixed Trokh with a bewildered amber gaze.

"But, Tolkhron... why? *Why?*" was all he could think to say. The man looked exultant, and that cut at Arcmas's heart like a dagger.

"For the purposes of the emperor – to serve him, and the people of his empire. It is what you were made for. Do you see now how foolish it is to question us? To try to consider some other way but ours?"

As far as Arcmas was concerned, that was the end of the interview. There may have been more the priest said, but the youth couldn't take it in. As though in a dream, he was somehow collected by the ambassador, handed over to Centenor Jakhron and then brought back to his cabin just outside the training camp, the place unbearably lonely now without Khaydon.

Now he picked up the quill pen once more and wrote four lines:

*I cannot even remember how I felt about everything before that priest told me that I was nobody; that I am just a monster made by magic. All of my thoughts before today seem foolish – they don't matter anymore. Why should I care so much about what I do or don't do? Only you and Father mean anything to me now.*

Then he laid aside his pen, dropping his head down onto his arms on the small table.

# Chapter Seventeen

Back at the Outpost, the same evening that Hennelyn was deciding to return home, Nik was playing the spy inside the house.

He had seen Ambassador Siras Thraulor arriving a few days before with all of his entourage and troops – over one hundred men! As usual, the Ambassador was housed in the chamber below Arcmas's old room. But Arcmas did not come with them. In fact, Centenor Jakhron had received the privilege of staying in Arcmas's bedroom in the upper half-story of the manor. Nik had heard that the Ambassador's proud little aide, Hanthor, had been displaced by a mere centenor - and relegated to a bunk among the ordinary men! Nik found that fact amusing.

Of course he was in and out of the Kanow house all the time, laying the fires in the four fireplaces and cleaning out the ashes. It was one of Nik's regular jobs. But this particular evening, he sensed something amiss, seeing the lanterns still on and many candles lit. Even more so when the general did not retire to bed but stayed up late with the Ambassador, Hanthor, Marshal Stokhor, and Centenor Jakhron, all seated around the table in the hall.

Risking a rebuke if found, Nik hid inside the house after lighting the evening fires, in Hennelyn's empty room. He sat on her bed in the dark. The Luinians Lisha and Jaero Lite retired, and probably his own family too. His brothers were no doubt asleep in the room he shared with them. Waiting in Hennelyn's bedchamber made him think of her. He had lost sleep this last week worrying for her safety. He'd missed her! But this room… it still smelled like her. He took a deep breath. A fresh scent lingered, like her hair, and he even thought he picked up a hint of the leafy balm she used to moisturize her skin.

The door was slightly open, and Nik could hear a little of what the men downstairs were discussing. It didn't sound very interesting. But then he heard a knock at the outer door. The men stopped droning on, falling into breathless silence. Then there were boots clunking across the floor towards the door. Nik took advantage of this noise to creep out of the room, kneeling down by the doorway in case someone glanced up. The upper story was gloomy, but he had to be careful.

Centenor Jakhron pulled open the door, and a robed figure came in. This new arrival paused inside the door while Jakhron shut it, to push the hood from his head. Nik stifled an involuntary gasp. Here, at last, was Arcmas! He had returned home after all.

As Arcmas followed Jakhron to the table, Nik stretched out full-length on the floor to peek between the balcony rails. The other four men rose slowly at Armas's approach. Nik could see the firelight gleam on the sweeping wing at this side, folded up tight, its tip brushing the floor. Nik had never seen him wear such a big, shapeless robe before. What was it for?

No one spoke as Arcmas saluted everyone smartly, halting near the Ambassador. Siras smiled at Tai's obvious surprise.

"Yes, General, this is the special recruit I was telling you about - the one we trained to solve our problems with these elusive bunjis. You didn't know that we were training him to help you, did you?"

It seemed to be an effort for Tai to answer.

"I... had hoped that Arcmas would prove to be a good soldier. Hello, Arcmas. Welcome home!"

His voice was warm. But Arcmas turned his yellow hawk eyes from Siras to Tai and returned his foster father's look coolly.

"Thank you, sir," he acknowledged politely. Had he grown? Nik couldn't really tell. The well-remembered lines of his face seemed thinner and harder. It had been almost six months since Nik had seen him last. Somehow Nik sensed that Arcmas had changed, but how, he didn't know.

Nik could see Siras's sharp features face-on; he seemed to be enjoying himself.

"Have you completed your task, Solit Arcmas?" the ambassador queried.

Arcmas ducked his head submissively. "I have, Your Excellency."

Siras's grey eyes gleamed.

"Show us!" he urged. At that, Arcmas opened his robe and pulled from within its folds a young bunji girl. She stumbled out onto her knees before them all. Her long straight hair, very black, was mussed from being tucked under the robe. She blinked in the light and swept the company with large, startled eyes. Nik jerked in surprise.

After a moment, Tai asserted quietly, "I assume that this is the apprentice, the young Adon Miru?"

"It is, sir," Arcmas answered, his voice oddly devoid of emotion.

"Stand her up, Arcmas," Siras broke in. "Let us see our prize better." When this was done, he mumbled, "What a strange creature. I haven't seen an Adon Miru for quite a while. They look so different from the others. Maybe they are like our albinos, except for the dark hair."

Her face was very pale and her eyes were blue, a pale shade that even Nik could see from where he lay. Her hair shimmered, long and black. She was perhaps sixteen years of age, smaller yet than Brinkle was, and gracefully slender. She wore the same basic buckskin clothing as the male bunjis, except that her tunic was longer and fringed at the hem, with what appeared to Nik to be embroidery stitched on its front. Over that she had on a long vest of silvery fur, unbuttoned, with an attached hood.

"They both look pale like this, Excellency, as you had informed me before," Arcmas volunteered. "This one and the old man - the former Adon Miru. *He* had white hair."

Siras shot him a sharp glance.

"And what was done with the old man?" he demanded.

"As per your orders, Your Excellency. He will never be seen again," came the chilling reply. Nik saw the young bunji shiver, as though she had understood the statement, though they were speaking the Starkhon language. Gooseflesh stippled Nik's arms too, in sympathy.

Then Siras addressed the girl directly in trade speech.

"Welcome to your new home, little one. You may have heard that we are not kind to our prisoners, but you yourself have nothing to fear. What do you suppose your people will think when they find that you have become our guest here?" She lifted her chin, and her clear, high voice hardly quivered as she spoke in accented tones.

"It doesn't matter that you have brought me here, sir. My people will not agree to become your slaves." *Surprisingly fluent*, Nik thought.

Siras leered and replied in his most caressing tone, "Well, I don't know if you can be so certain of that yet. Now that we have you. What are you called, child?"

No answer. There was a pause as Siras and the girl measured each other up.

"She's a brave one, Your Excellency," Arcmas remarked in Starkhonese with some amusement. "She didn't show much fear of me when I came to collect her."

"How did you find her, Solit Arcmas?"

"I did just as you said, sir. I watched all the bunji movements for miles around. Soon enough, one of them led me to the hiding place of the Adon Mirus. They were in a large cave on the side of the riverbank far west of here, where it rises as high as a cliff, reached only by a rope ladder which they pulled up behind them. I guess they didn't plan for an enemy that could fly."

He sounded smug and cold, not like himself at all.

"Well done, Solit. I knew you would be an asset to us. I expect the general is proud as well."

"Indeed," Tai said slowly and rather sadly, to Nik's ears.

Siras turned to Tai and boasted, "One problem solved. We may now get on with the rest of the agenda."

"Yes, Excellency. I suppose that the first thing is to place this youngster in the east tower under heavy guard. We need to collect men from the barracks. My guards or yours, sir?"

"It does not matter. Whoever is best suited. But Solit Arcmas, did you search the prisoner for weapons?"

"Yes, Your Excellency. She has none."

"Very well. Let us all go see her installed straight away. I, too, am looking forward to a good night's rest," Siras remarked.

He walked toward the door, still talking, and everyone else followed, forcing the bunji girl along with them. They all filed out and slammed the door shut.

Nik let his breath out slowly. For a long moment he was afraid to move. *A good decision,* he thought a moment later, as he heard the muffled thumps of two doors below him shutting tighter. The two Luinians downstairs had also been listening. Now he had to get out, before anyone returned to catch him.

# Chapter Eighteen

The next morning, Hennelyn set out east alone, leaving her new friends. She refused the offer of even one of them coming along with her. She would not endanger any more of them than she had to, especially if there were two Adon Mirus waiting for her rescue back home.

She walked out on the bald prairie for quite a while to distance herself from any of the camps that she had used before. In the middle of the afternoon she finally came to a halt. Here she built a small fire and shook the powder on it which would make the smoke turn a bright orange, to signal the patrols that were nearest to pick her up.

It did not take long. Just under two hours had passed when a three-man mounted patrol came over the bare rise in the east and approached. The fitful sun under scudding clouds picked out the gleam of their helmets and the shiny gold mane of the lightest-colored horse.

Hennelyn stamped out the fire as they approached. These were men she knew by their faces but not by name. The nearest one held a hand out to her without a word, and she grasped it with her good arm to clumsily mount up behind his saddle. She had only just that day abandoned her sling. He squeezed the horse to set it in motion, just a walk, and she was on her slow way home. One of the men peeled off at a quicker pace and left the other two behind; he would no doubt give warning of her return before she arrived. The other two riders took turns trotting and walking, saving the strength of the horse with the extra burden of Hennelyn's weight.

The distance was greater than Hennelyn had realized. They ate a little from the saddle bags as they went, and they only made short stops in the daytime to eat and let the horses graze. That night they only rested twice for a maximum of three hours each, snatching a little sleep.

By the time it was dark on the second interminable day of traveling, they were finally within the environs of the Outpost. It was dark all around, but the horses knew their way. Hennelyn was resting wearily against the back of the man in front of her when her surroundings began to look familiar. They were just starting to climb the long hill to her family home. Her heart quickened like a drum roll announcing her arrival.

The gate into the compound was manned. It opened and closed for her and her escort. Ahead of her the yard lay still and quiet; she could see the ghostly shapes of the new soldier's tents clogging the open spaces. But what riveted her gaze was the backlit figure standing in the dim amber rectangle of the house's open door.

The horses drew nearer, and Hennelyn identified her father. The other horseman parted company with them and headed for the stables, but her rider brought her right to the door of her home where she slid down into Tai's strong arms. Her eyes pricked at the sight of his solemn but relieved face. She thought he looked older than she remembered. Or maybe thinner? He said nothing but guided her into the house with a gentle arm around her shoulder. The fire was still banked up a little in the fireplace, casting the glow she had seen from outside. He shut the door and guided her inside.

"You will be weary. They've laid the fire in your room," was all he said. But his hand trembled on her back as they climbed the stairs together. He stopped at her door, folding her into his arms. His beard tickled as he spoke quietly into her ear.

"I am so glad you are home again… my dear daughter." And there he left her to enter her own little room where one candle burned to bid her welcome, the flame elongating and swimming in the tears falling from her eyes.

The next morning Hennelyn woke late, feeling grimy and greasy-headed. She was very grateful when the maid Dewdra brought her breakfast in bed - scrambled eggs and sausage meat and hot bread, and even a cup of hot hop! A merry blaze in the fireplace warmed the room. It felt like the lap of luxury after all those days of rough living.

Dewdra greeted her with enthusiasm, breathlessly glad to see her, and Hennelyn asked for the tub to be filled for her in the kitchen. She was aching for a hot bath and a hair wash.

"Of course, Mistress Hennelyn – it will be ready when you are!" Dewdra said brightly.

Later Hennelyn went out to the kitchen in a bathrobe and boots, carrying clean clothes against her chest. In front of the fireplace in the kitchen a large, three-paneled wooden screen was set up to make a private space before the warm blaze. Hennelyn kicked off her boots, handed her robe to Dewdra, and stepped bare into the big metal tub, steaming with warm water. It was just deep enough to reach Hennelyn's waist as she sat down, but when she leaned into the angle of the back, then the water covered her to the neck.

Dewdra washed Hennelyn's hair first, wrapping it in the towel and leaving her to soak in private a little. If the maid noticed Hennelyn's bandaged arm, she did not remark on it. It felt heavenly to Hennelyn to soap off the grime of sleeping rough for more than a week.

The bandage softened in the water, and Hennelyn pulled it off to examine the wound. The skin around it looked close to its usual color, and the round punctures were smaller and shallower now. Poking at them elicited only a slight tenderness. She didn't think her arm needed any more wrapping. Dewdra returned a little later to help her dry off and dress.

As she left the screen freshly dressed, the kitchen ladies smiled at her, and she saw that Nik and little Winellika had come there to greet her. Hennelyn actually blushed under Nik's wide smile of welcome. He looked so glad to see her.

"Well, let's get your hair brushed," Dewdra said, sitting her down on a bench. "Your father and His Excellency will soon be ready for lunch, and they will want you to join them, even if you don't need to eat yet, after such a late breakfast. Everyone is very glad you are back safe and sound from your wilderness week."

*So that's the official story,* Hennelyn thought. *Father must have succeeded in hiding my treason.*

Dewdra unwound the towel from Hennelyn's head and began to brush out the tangles. Winellika sat close to admire the operation and carried on a little childish conversation with her. Nik said little, merely watching. The noise of the kitchen and talk of the ladies was good cover for his tongue-tied state.

She returned to the main house on her own, knowing the cooks would soon follow her over with the food. The cool air chilled her wet head as she walked. Her heartbeat quickened as she approached the house. Had Siras Thraulor been told anything about Brinkle and his escape yet? Would Arcmas be there? Would she be allowed to see the new captives? There were so many unknowns. Well, there was nothing to be done now but to face up to the household and Siras. She drew a deep breath and opened the door of the manor.

No one really noticed her as she first entered. She saw the Ambassador and his aide Hanthor seated there with Tai Kanow - only the three of them.

Her father saw her approach first, and he did a strange thing.

He stood up out of his seat, and gathered her to his side as she drew close.

"Ah, my daughter joins us," he remarked warmly.

"Mistress Hennelyn," Siras greeted her. Hanthor echoed him.

"Your Excellency. Sir Hanthor," she returned politely. Then Tai did something else unusual. He called the Luinians out of their rooms.

"It is my daughter's first meal back with us; her governess and tutor ought to join us," he explained. Hennelyn received a tender hug from both Jaero Lite and Lisha. They held back their tears with heroic effort. It was apparent that *they* knew more than the 'official story' and were greatly relieved to see her.

"She seems to have come well through her wilderness week," remarked Siras with an appraising glance. "And soon it will be your coming of age celebration. April fifteenth, is it?" Though her head was spinning with relief, Hennelyn only nodded politely in affirmation and everyone sat, shortly followed by the cooks with lunch.

Hennelyn picked at some bread and fielded a few polite questions about her adventure. Since no one there was really telling the truth except Siras, the conversation struggled, and the others wisely kept their questions to a minimum.

Fortunately, Siras's thoughts appeared to be elsewhere.

"This Adon Miru apprentice is an interesting creature," he told them. "I had thought that she would be childish and dull, but she is wise beyond her years, it seems. And she has no difficulty understanding the trade speech and answering, though her accent is strong. For instance, did you know, General, that usually only the Adon Mirus among the bunjis learn to read and write?"

"No, I didn't," Tai replied. "Although I do remember you mentioning something about the Sacred Scrolls, or some such thing."

"Yes. But Arcmas did not report any sign of those. I have, however, once seen a partial copy of them. Years ago."

"What kind of spirits did you find the prisoner in this morning?" Tai asked him.

"The guards told me she had wept a little. I suppose she mourns her mentor, the old Adon Miru."

Hennelyn's heart jumped.

"What's wrong with the old one?" she burst out, unable to help herself.

Tai looked uncomfortable, but Siras answered calmly, "Arcmas's orders were to dispose of the older one and bring us only the apprentice."

Hennelyn blinked rapidly, appalled. Her brother had actually been ordered to kill one of the bunjis? The older Adon Miru? *Does Grogo know?* she wondered. *And Fraeling, and Brinkle? They will be devastated!*

Siras went on, taking no notice, "Yet she talked to me calmly enough. She has an air of wanting to please us, but I find that there are many things that she will not give a definite reply to. She always gives an answer, but many of them are like riddles - with little meaning."

Hennelyn blurted, "Father, where is Arcmas? Isn't he here too? I am anxious to see him."

With an edge to his voice over her rude interruption, Siras answered instead. "His time with your family is over, young mistress. He is a full-fledged soldier now." He smiled briefly at the unintended pun. "He is trained for our personal use from now on."

Hennelyn said nothing, silently berating herself for losing control of her emotion, especially in full view of the ambassador. But Siras added without concern, "If you are looking for a formal good-bye, I will see what I can arrange for the two of you in a little while."

Hennelyn said nothing more until lunch was over and she could escape.

Later that afternoon, Arcmas met up with the ambassador, Tai Kanow, and Solit Nakhanor at the tower holding the Adon Miru. It looked exactly the same as when Brinkle had stayed there, except that this time there was a small wooden screen in front of the bucket by the fireplace. As they all climbed up into the tower, they found the prisoner on her knees in front of the square open window, staring up at it. The day was warm, but there was still a low fire smouldering in the fireplace.

Arcmas felt a flush of heat climb up the back of his neck and head as he looked at the slight young girl, remembering the night he had invaded their hideout and carried her off. But she did not appear to notice that he or anyone else was even there. Her pale skin seemed to almost glow so that she was circled by a faint aura. The men all hesitated, staring at her. She stayed completely still.

"She's at it again," muttered the ambassador, his thin lips twisting. Nakhanor stirred.

"Shall I put her in the chair, Your Excellency?" he asked. Siras gave a short sardonic laugh.

"You can try if you wish, Solit, but you won't be able to get near her. I warn you, this pose means that she is practicing some kind of black magic. I discovered how it operates this morning."

Nakhanor moved towards the bunji. But he went only two steps before he faltered and stopped dead. Siras nodded in triumph.

"I told you so."

"Solit Nakhanor, continue!" ordered Tai. But the hefty soldier only stood there, and made a kind of strangled noise.

"Let Arcmas try," Siras suggested. The youth strode up next to Nakhanor and peered sideways at his face. The expression on it made a shiver pass down his spine. Nakhanor stood as though he were paralysed, his face red with effort. He did not react to Arcmas's presence.

With a puzzled frown, the youth approached the girl himself. He managed to get close enough to touch her, but as he leaned down to take her by the arm, his body also froze. He stood like a statue in his bent posture. Fear fluttered in his belly as he seemed unable to move either forward or back. This hadn't happened the night he'd captured her! From his frozen position he had a clear view of the girl's face.

It was lifted up like a flower seeking the sun. Her blue eyes were wide open and sparkling. The corners of her mouth turned up slightly, and though her expression was serene, Arcmas was struck by the thought that he had never seen so much joy in a face before. She seemed to glow with it. As the natural outdoor light fell on her, Arcmas saw that her pale skin was so translucent that he could see the red and blue shades of her blood coming and going from her heart, just under the smooth surface, like alabaster coming to life.

She took no notice of him, staring straight ahead as though in a trance. Arcmas felt a strong desire to speak to her, to touch her, but a great reluctance seemed to grip him at the same time, as though it would be somehow profane to disturb this.

As Arcmas hovered over the little bunji, she broke the spell herself by shutting her dark-lashed eyes and bowing her head. When she moved again, it was to look up into Arcmas's face with a puzzled, but patient gaze. He felt an odd release. Now he could reach a hand down to her.

"Adon Miru, allow me to help you up," he murmured in the trade speech, wondering as he spoke why he felt the need to address her so politely all of a sudden. She readily put her small hand in his, and he pulled her to her feet and led her to the chair. She perched on its edge and looked around at the other men curiously.

"Congratulations, Solit Arcmas," noted the ambassador dryly, "you are the only one I've seen get anywhere near this prisoner when

143

she is fully into her sorcery. Although I notice that even you could not touch her until she allowed it. Now if we may continue...?" He looked pointedly at Nakhanor, who approached the chair rather shame-faced. Arcmas retreated.

"Why do we need the serum?" Tai asked, as he saw the darts Nakhanor carried. "We do not need any information from her, do we? I thought she was merely a hostage to force the cooperation of the local bunjis."

"I will be the judge of that, General," was Siras's curt answer.

The young bunji girl watched Nakhanor anxiously, knowing that the darts were for her, but she didn't struggle when the solit took up her slender arm in his strong grasp. She closed her eyes and turned her face away during the administration of the drug.

Tai suddenly said, "Don't be afraid, child, this won't hurt you."

She opened her turquoise eyes and fixed her gaze on him.

Then they waited. Finally it occurred to Ambassador Thraulor that they had been waiting too long for some effect. The girl watched them, showing no signs of anything but some bafflement.

"It appears that the drug is not working," mused Siras with a slight edge to his words. Everyone waited a few minutes more.

"Your Excellency, I believe you are right," Tai agreed at last.

"Perhaps we should increase the dosage."

"We don't know if that would be safe. She's just a child."

Siras's lips pressed together impatiently, turning them white. "Then I will remain here and talk to the prisoner without the aid of the drug for now. But Solit - we shall make another attempt with the serum tomorrow, and I will expect it to be done right."

Nakhanor cleared his throat, but his answer still came out hoarse. "Yes, your Excellency."

Siras looked down his narrow nose at the man, who saluted and scurried out. When Nakhanor had disappeared down the ladder, Tai turned back to the Ambassador.

"Do you need Arcmas and I to stay with you any longer, sir?"

"I should think not. Arcmas, you are dismissed back to your base to await further orders. General, could you help her out of the chair before you go? I wish to sit down myself. The child and I will have a little visit all on our own, I believe."

Arcmas saluted, turning away. He saw Tai gently pull the bunji out of the chair so that Siras could sit down. The last thing Arcmas saw before climbing through the trapdoor was the two of them, the fresh, blooming face of the young girl in a standoff opposite the thin, pointed features of the ambassador, so grey and lined. Her head was only slightly above the level of his, though he was seated. To Arcmas's mind, the scene looked like that of a little bird standing hypnotized before the coiled threat of a serpent.

As he stepped off the bottom rung, he heard Siras say coolly, "Now, child, shall we take up where we left off this morning? And do add a few more details, my dear."

General Kanow's legs appeared as he began to descend the ladder, so Arcmas rushed off to avoid being alone in the room with his foster father.

Hennelyn spent that first day home restless and impatient. She was holed up most of the time with Lisha and Dewdra. Siras's convoy had brought along some fine new material, soft and fleecy teal green cloth, as well as some slithery golden stuff. The ladies were anxious to get new clothes made for Hennelyn, feminine clothes that would be more like Lisha's robes than Hennelyn's boyish tunics and leggings. Though she was patient with the day of measuring and pinning, she ached to have some time alone to think. The new captive had to be rescued, and no one but Hennelyn herself was there to do it. Also, she really wanted to ask Nik for advice, since her mind stubbornly refused to come up with a plan.

Finally the opportunity came when he brought in the wood after supper for the evening fires. No one was overly surprised when Hennelyn bolted from the supper table to follow him up to her room. They were friends, after all.

As soon as she followed him into her room, they fell into an embrace, each hugging the other tightly.

"I missed you *so much!*" Nik croaked into the honey-golden hair at her neck. All of the aromas he had noticed faintly before now filled his nostrils in full strength. She was similarly struck by his strong outdoorsy smell and his slender but wiry frame.

"I missed you too, Nik. Every bit as much!"

They released each other, and both noted the dampness in the other's blue eyes; Nik's blue lighter, Hennelyn's deeper and more like the vault above a hot summer day. This led to a bit of nervous giggling between them and helped banish their first awkwardness.

Then Hennelyn remarked solemnly, "It must have been awful for you to be left behind to bear the gossip and suspicion about me."

"Oh, it wasn't allowed. Your father told everyone it was your 'wilderness week,' and he would not stand for any connection between you and the bunji's escape to be even whispered aloud - by anyone. Not in *his* hearing."

"And he hasn't said anything at all to the ambassador about Brinkle being here? Or have any other of our soldiers mentioned it to him?"

"Not that I've heard. I've been listening hard around our own soldiers. I've heard the word 'traitor'…" Nik whispered the terrible word, "but so far I haven't heard anyone dare mention your name. Everyone came completely unlaced in this house after you left. You should have seen how your father's face looked for days afterward. And Lisha and Jaero Lite – all trying to pretend that they were not terrified for you."

Hennelyn hugged him again. "I'm sorry. You must have been so worried."

He swallowed and nodded. "Yes. My whole family was. Even though they trusted your father."

She stepped over to her bed and slowly sank down on it. Her heart quickened its rhythm at the mention of her father.

"This is a dangerous game – this one my father is playing. Siras is bound to hear of it sooner or later. I have to act quickly."

Nik paled visibly. He also came to the bed, but he plopped down hard beside her as though his legs had given out.

"What do you mean by that? 'Act quickly?'" he queried nervously.

"With the Adon Miru, of course! I need to get her out of this place before everything is discovered and it's too late!"

Nik nervously rubbed a hand over his face.

"I can't find any way to tell you… how *terrified* I've been that you would say exactly that!" He turned wide eyes on her.

"Yet you knew I would."

"I hoped you wouldn't. It's impossible, anyway!" Nik gestured wildly. "Security is tighter this time. Only Siras and your father are allowed into the tower from now on, besides the double guards. And Nakhanor when they want him. You won't get near the prisoner now – especially not you. The door to the outside is barred, which it wasn't before. No one could get into that tower without a set of wings."

She glanced at him sharply. He saw an idea dawning like little double suns in her gaze.

*"Without a set of wings..."* she breathed. "Genius, Nik!"

"What?" he said. Then horrified incredulity dawned. "Are you thinking what I think you are? No, Henna! Arcmas is a soldier now!"

"But it's perfect! Arcmas is the only one who could get into that tower now. Even if the window were closed, he could get in," she said, not knowing that he'd already been there earlier that day.

"But *he's* the one who captured her in the first place! He would never be persuaded to get her out, even by us. He's... he's not the same boy anymore, Hennelyn. I know. I saw him that night, when he brought the little Adon Miru here. Don't you know?" His voice fell to a whisper. "He *killed* the other Adon Miru."

Silence thumped down between them. For a long shocked minute, only the hissing of the flames was heard. Nik rose and went over to the fire to poke new life into it, but mostly because he didn't want Hennelyn to see how angry he was at Arcmas. He merely stirred the coals listlessly around. Hennelyn stood to pace around the small footage of her room, thinking hard.

After a few minutes, she stopped and stared at Nik's stooping, dejected back.

"Do you even know where Arcmas is?" she asked softly.

"I... I think he is staying out by Springs Falls. I've watched his hawk fly that way to take him his orders."

"His orders!" Hennelyn exclaimed. She quickly walked to Nik and grabbed him by his arms to face her. "What orders?"

"His written orders from the ambassador. The ambassador writes them out for him, passes them on to Centenor Jakhron in an envelope, and then Jakhron attaches them to the hawk and sends them out. At least, that's what I've assumed they do. I've been watching all of them every day while you were gone. They got here the day after you left."

A grateful tear slid down Hennelyn's cheek, and she hugged him yet again.

"Oh Nik! Thank you for being so clever and observant. What would I ever do without you?" She added quietly, "You're my best friend."

He smiled.

"And you are mine," was his answer. "Always."

147

"And now I need some time. You've given me a lot to think about!"

Nik left her doing just that, staring straight in front of her. Somehow what he said had provided the grist for the mill of her inventive mind. He wondered a bit nervously what the result would be.

# Chapter Nineteen

If there really was an Adon out there in the ether somewhere, perhaps it was due to his intervention that after a mere four days at home (and the fifth day of the Adon Miru's capture), Hennelyn escaped her 'house arrest' and was now standing outside on a moonless night just below freezing, with light snow nestling onto her hair and melting into little icy rills down her neck. This time, Nik was there right beside her, his breath smoking up into the starry sky. They were accompanied by a dozen bunjis.

She would not soon forget how Nik had suddenly materialized beside her earlier this same night, as she had been tossing the rope up to go over the wall. He'd been all packed up and ready to go along. His low, fierce whisper had convinced her of his resolve when she'd tried to turn him back: "You left without me once," he had hissed in the darkness, "but you won't do it again!"

Without Nik, she would not have found a way out for the young Adon Miru. Nik had been right, as usual; she had not been allowed near the new prisoner at any time. It had been Nik who'd smuggled her the copy of Siras Thraulor's written orders, then re-smuggled Hennelyn's replacements back into the guestroom. Once, he was almost caught as he stood over Siras's bedchamber table, just after slipping the false orders into the envelope. He had risked his life doing so, but thankfully Siras had not been suspicious enough to check the orders before handing them off to Jakhron after supper. Nik had only been rebuked and banned from entering Siras's chamber again.

In the end, it was also Nik's skillful toss that had set the rope over one pared-off wooden point of the wall for them to climb out and over. They had had to leave the rope behind, with the hope that it would not be discovered until they were long gone.

Now a crowd of onlookers, bunji and human, breathlessly waited near the Spring Falls, about two miles from the Outpost, to see if Arcmas and the Adon Miru would turn up.

They had been waiting for about an hour, but Hennelyn's adrenaline was still at high tide, throbbing through her veins. From that

149

night on, her future was a blank in which anything could happen, and she was more than a little nervous. She felt totally bereft of any ability to plot and plan anymore, if she should fail this time.

Afraid to think too far ahead, she replayed their escape in her mind instead, recalling each scene of the evening, a few hours ago:

After supper, the Luinians played a board game at another table nearer the opposite wall, and the lighthearted voices lent a familiar homey cheerfulness to the room. Hennelyn and her father sat at the table, talking in front of the fire. She'd been relishing these last moments, not knowing if or when she would see her father, or any of them, again, when Siras came out of his room, dragging Nik by the arm. Then followed the unpleasant scene of Nik's tongue-lashing and subsequent ignominious banishment from any space which also contained the ambassador; he was then sent off to the servant's hall.

After that, Siras approached her and her father, saying, "Well, I do hope I didn't interrupt a sentimental discussion between father and daughter." Hennelyn recalled quenching a spasm of anger at his mocking tone.

"We were only talking of my early soldiering days," Tai assured him. "Hennelyn wanted to hear some of the old stories again. I must take every opportunity I can to pass these tales on, especially when it's my daughter asking me. She never wanted to hear them as often as Arcmas used to, when he was small." He sounded wistful as he said this. Hennelyn realized then, with a shock, that he was missing Arcmas as much as she was. *Was he nearby - or not? Would he ever rejoin their family?* Hennelyn wondered just what she would find out about him a few hours later, if everything went as planned.

Later that evening, when all was still, Hennelyn readied herself to leave. By the light of a small candle, she dressed warmly. She reached under her bed to retrieve the rope that she had stashed there a couple of days before and experienced a sudden sense of déjà vu. Here she was, once again creeping out with a rope in her hand! But just before she left, she placed one envelope with a short letter inside it on her night stand, addressed to her father, and another epistle inside the only drawer, addressed to Lisha and Jaero Lite. She hoped each would eventually make it to the proper hands.

After stumbling across Nik, determined to join her, the two of them climbed the wall with little trouble, in spite of the loud scrape of boots on wood. At the top, they pulled up the rope, hesitating to throw it down the other side until they knew whether a guard was patrolling nearby. No sign of one yet.

As they set down outside the wall, a dog started to bark, not far around the corner of the fence from where they stood. Hearts racing, they turned and ran out into the night. A large distance of bare ground had to be crossed before they could reach any cover. Hennelyn was inclined to give the two of them up for lost even as she ran beside Nik. But then something odd happened.

Only a few steps ahead and to the right of them, part of the ground's surface seemed to peel away and rise up vertically, creating a dark cave under a lid of turf. They heard a quick hiss from inside it, and a hand stuck out of the shadows, gesturing urgently for them to come. Startled as they were by this sudden apparition, Nik and Hennelyn immediately went towards it. As they drew nearer, they saw an unfamiliar bunji standing in a deep hole. The two youngsters jumped into this pit feet first. They were barely in time. As soon as they were in, the top of the enclosure came down almost on their heads. It didn't close completely; the bunji had left a crack to see what was happening outside, so that Nik and Hennelyn had a view of the guard as he was pulled around the corner at a dead run by his dog's leash.

At first, the dog loped directly towards their hiding place, but the bunji with them pursed his lips in a strange way. Hennelyn didn't hear any sound, but the dog shook his head, hesitated, and then ran suddenly off to the west away from them. His barking faded into the distance as the three occupants listened, wedged together in the narrow space. They were safe.

The bunji kept them there for some minutes, giving Hennelyn a chance to investigate the hole. She couldn't see much, of course, but she smelled an aroma of plant material and freezing soil. The depression was lined with something both above and below them. *Probably juniper,* she thought, by the smell. She took off a glove and felt above her head. There seemed to be an interlocking grid of slender wooden poles there to support the turf over them. That explained why it opened and closed in one piece.

"So this is how!" Hennelyn whispered in suppressed excitement, switching to the trade language.

"How what?" Nik asked in the same tongue.

"This is how the bunjis disappear so quickly when we chase them! There must be hundreds of these little pockets in the ground all over for hiding in!"

"You are right," confirmed the bunji beside her. "There are

many of these, especially near the houses of the Fierce Ones. Your men often run right over us and never know we are here."

"Wow!" Nik and Hennelyn said together. "To think that we never even suspected such a thing," Hennelyn added.

"Yes, but now it is time for us to go," the bunji said. "That soldier could return." He pushed up the lid, and the three of them climbed slowly out of the hole. The bunji pointed north.

"Go that way, children. Follow the lights. We have been watching for your escape and all is ready," he whispered urgently. As they turned and started to jog away, they heard him murmur, "Adon go with you."

They moved quickly until they reached the coulee. When they were down among the trees, they saw a tiny light flickering ahead of them. And then another. Many bunjis must be stationed out there, using their tinderbox matches to light a path for them. The youngsters traveled as quickly as they could through thick copses of trees, following the valley basically north as it twisted back and forth.

After a while, another unexpected thing happened. They heard the soft nicker of a horse from the shadow beneath some trees at the final small light. She and Nik slowed to a walk. They found two horses there, wearing only makeshift halters, each held by a bunji keeper. Even in the gloom under the trees, they could see white teeth gleaming through black beards. A soft male voice greeted them.

"Ah... you come at last! For days we have 'borrowed' horses, different ones each time to make no one suspicious while we waited for you. Take these horses now and ride them to the start of the next valley. Enter it, and you will find Laero Grogo waiting at the end of the coulee on the plain. You will see his torch. Hurry now!"

The two youngsters thanked the speaker, grateful that they would not have to run anymore. Hennelyn had already felt a stitch growing in her side, and her newly healed arm was a little sore from climbing the wall.

Nik gave her a leg-up onto her bareback mount, and the bunji did the same for him. Soon they were cantering side by side. It would not take long now to complete the first phase of their escape, though they knew they were racing against time. Rising up against the stars before them loomed the shoulders of the highest Signpost Hill.

Twenty minutes later they were over it, their journey shortened by the speed of the horses. As quickly as they could, allowing their mounts to pick a way through, they climbed down among spruce and underbrush. Soon they came out into the valley to see a small meadow bottom nestled between shallow ridges. A little ways north against the trees, they saw a steady torch burning, larger than the small lights the bunji guides had been using. They turned the horses towards it and rapidly closed in.

At the further edge of this meadow, backed by a thick belt of spruce trees, was where they'd found a group of about twelve bunjis, all of them muffled in white and brown, mottled like the terrain. They stood as silent and still as statues as the newcomers approached. One of them held the torch. Not even a gleam of an eye escaped the shadow of their hoods. As Nik and Hennelyn stopped in front of them, two of the silent figures stepped forward. The first hood pushed back revealed Grogo, regarding them with a broad grin.

"Welcome, Henlin!" he'd said. "You are here at last. It has been hard to wait for you while our little Adon Miru sits in your prison tower. But we have been watching."

With an answering smile, Hennelyn slid off of the horse and approached him. They clasped each other in a bear hug.

"Grogo, it's so good to see you! Thanks for trusting me."

"Is everything going according to plan? Where is the Adon Miru now?" the bunji queried.

"I don't know. We'll find out very soon."

To banish uncomfortable thoughts of possible failure, she turned to the figure behind the laero.

"Who's this?" she teased. She already knew, even before he removed his hood, that the shorter bunji there was Brinkle. He also smiled at her, showing his very white teeth, his dark eyes sparkling. He too had a hug for her. Many more hoods came down then, revealing more welcoming faces. Fraeling had come, and Tuppin too. They clasped forearms with Hennelyn and then approached Nik for introductions in their easy, accepting way. Brinkle then shyly touched Hennelyn's wounded arm.

"Very much better now," he remarked solemnly.

"Yes. Thanks to you two and Fraeling. I've really missed you all."

"And us, you," Grogo reassured her. "But what happens now, Henlin?" She could not suppress a stomach flutter over this question.

"If everything goes right, they should be arriving soon." These words occasioned some bewilderment among the bunjis, as they looked at one another and muttered together in their own language.

"They?" Grogo wondered.

"Someone I know is bringing her, I hope," was Hennelyn's reply. "Did you all bring some of your sleeping potion and darts? The ones you had before, when the mountain lion attacked me?"

Grogo reassured her that they still had these things.

"But Henlin, why should we need them?" he asked.

"We might need to knock someone out - but only long enough to tie him up. I... I want a chance to talk to him. You'll be able to do that?"

"Of course. But how many do you expect?"

"Just one," she murmured. Grogo exchanged another glance with his men.

He said carefully, "Then you are expecting this one guard to be hostile to us when he arrives? He is not part of your rescue plan?"

Hennelyn squirmed.

"No - not willingly. He doesn't know that it's us waiting for him. I guess... I don't know yet. That's why I want to talk to him. To offer him the choice of joining us." Grogo smoothed his beard in thought.

"Would we be talking of the Aesthe?" he asked perceptively. When Hennelyn nodded, Grogo added, "Do you think it wise to try to talk to him? Would it not be better to knock him out right away and make our escape while he is sleeping?"

Hennelyn shrugged in frustration.

"I don't know! I don't know if it's wise. I just - I haven't been able to see him or speak to him at all, and I... I just have to try."

She looked at him beseechingly. Grogo met her eyes intently, but if he was thinking she was being foolish, he had the grace not to say so. After a moment he nodded and broke their gaze.

"Thank you, Laero Grogo," she said softly.

So now, long after midnight, they were all waiting together for whatever happened next, most probably feeling as much suspense as Hennelyn herself. She couldn't escape some worried thoughts that kept niggling at the back of her mind.

*If Arcmas does come, will he be followed by all of the soldiers of the Outpost? They are over four miles away but not too far to catch us if they take horses. And if he doesn't come - what will I do then?*

She sighed and stamped her feet. The cold was beginning to bite into her toes as they all stood, unmoving, in the meadow. One or two owls hooted nearby. One of the horses she and Nik had ridden snorted, loud in the tense silence. Hennelyn found herself crossing her fingers. If this didn't work, there was no going back and no opportunity to try again. This was her only chance.

A light breeze stirred, ruffling her hair. In the same moment, the moon kicked off part of its blanket of cloud. Everyone's breath plumed in the fresh silver light; the torch had been put out some time before. The bunjis around her all pulled their hoods up again against the wind. Then Hennelyn thought she saw a dark shape flit quickly across the white specks of the stars, blotting them out briefly.

"Did you see that?" she whispered to Grogo.

"Probably just an owl," he whispered back. But Hennelyn shook her head. She pulled her own hood on, then took the extinguished torch from the bunji who held it and walked a few steps away from the group.

All at once, there came a sudden extra gust, and something descended rapidly from the sky above them, a huge silhouette edged with revealing moonlight. It landed just a little way out from them where the valley was bare of trees.

There was enough moonlight to see one small figure disentangle from the larger one. Huge shadowy wings folded up and shrank the larger figure to a more reasonable size. Hennelyn walked out into the valley towards these two newcomers, her heart beating as though it would break free of its cage of bone. Then she heard his voice, lifted up confidently, assured of welcome and approval.

"Centenor Jakhron? Ambassador Thraulor? Is that you?"

It had been so long since she'd heard Arcmas speak! She thrilled with both affection and apprehension from head to toe. *Careful now!* It was imperative that she not startle him into flight.

Without answering, she lifted the dead torch and relit it with a scratch of her own tinderbox match. The others were far enough back under the shadow of the trees that Hennelyn was confident that Arcmas could not yet see them in spite of the torch. It sputtered into full flame and threw back the darkness surrounding the three people there.

A long moment went by as Arcmas and the young bunji girl squinted at her in the sudden light. Then recognition burst from Arcmas in a hoarse whisper.

"Hennelyn!"

He'd left so many months ago. Now Hennelyn was looking at her brother as though for the first time, seeing him as the bunjis must be seeing him, like a hallucination, an impossible creature with those great pinions, those curving talons - all those feathers. Yet, despite the

H.M. Richardson

slightly sharper angles it had gained, his face was as familiar to her as her own, as loved as ever.

He was wearing full field gear, his helmet balanced over his face, but it could not hide his youth. Riveted by astonishment, his mouth dropped open. Then he demanded, "What are you doing here? I... I thought..."

His words dribbled away, and he swallowed hard.

"Hello, Arcmas, my brother. Aren't you glad to see me?"

With annoyance, Hennelyn heard a pitiful ghost of her usual voice come out of her mouth as she asked this. Arcmas glanced uneasily into the darkness behind her. With his animal-sharp senses, he knew right away that she was not alone.

"Did you come with the soldiers? Did you bring the general?"

He was still bewildered. The perfect time for her to make the first move.

"Is this the Adon Miru?" Hennelyn asked him. She strode forward quickly, hand outstretched as though for a shake. "It's nice to meet you. I am General Kanow's daughter, Hennelyn," she said in the common tongue.

The young female bunji, who had been watching this exchange in wary silence, seemed to have gotten an instant grasp of the situation. She stepped quickly away from Arcmas and grasped Hennelyn's hand strongly.

"Hello. I am the Adon Miru's apprentice. You can call me Laria."

Just like that, the captive was out of Arcmas's control and into Hennelyn's. The sound of rushing feet swelled behind her. With one strong pivot, Hennelyn swung the smaller girl back behind her, into the arms of her people, who now flanked Hennelyn, bristling with spears. The element of surprise had worked, but not for long. Arcmas saw right away that this crowd was not the one he had expected. His gemstone eyes hardened in the torchlight, and his posture immediately stiffened with menace. But he did not attack, not yet. Instead, he tore a piece of paper from his uniform breast pocket.

"But why? Do you mean to tell me – this is a *trick?* And that you...?"

He threw the paper at her feet. She recognized it, of course. It was her counterfeit order. She had written it in as close a hand to Siras's as she could get. It had been difficult, so the orders were succinct.

*Solit Arcmas, there is a traitor suspected in the compound who will try to break the Adon Miru out of the tower tonight. Do not trust anyone, even the tower guards. Get her out through the window and bring her to the Spring Falls meadow at midnight. We will meet you there. Signed, Ambassador Thraulor*

"I'm sorry, Arcmas. It was the only way I could think of to get both of you here tonight," she apologized.

"There were rumors," he muttered. "Rumors that there was an earlier bunji capture, and a traitor that rescued him. We were going to follow it up... right away."

His eyes widened with disbelief and anger. With a swift movement, a large blade flashed out of his scabbard, reflecting sparks of torchlight.

"It's you! You are the traitor!" he yelled.

He flowed swiftly into action, but before the blade touched anyone, a dart smacked him full in the forehead. He brushed it away, and his wings snapped open, picking him up off the ground. He swooped down on them like a winged fury, scattering everyone. Someone parried his mighty stroke with a ringing of metal on metal. That bunji fell under the blow but seemed unharmed. Another one engaged and prevented the skewering of the fallen one. But the battle was short-lived. The dart had already delivered its dose.

Arcmas faltered, stumbling on his feet. He sank suddenly to one knee. The bunjis all drew back. Blood trickled from the small round gouge above his feathery brows. He stared around at them and blinked once, slowly. Then his eyes found Hennelyn once more. He gazed at her in terrible reproach and comprehension of what was happening to him. She saw fear in his eyes for the first time; he was definitely feeling the effects of the drugged dart. Sleepiness wiped away the fierceness of his expression, and he looked again like the brother he had been months before.

The giant wings spread. *Was he going to get away after all?* Hennelyn wondered. At first, it seemed he might. He rose into the air ponderously, and flew without his usual grace straight into the top of a spruce tree behind all of them. Everyone spun to track his movements. He clung there a moment, shaking his head hard to clear it, and spread his wings once more to the air. But it was only to float down like a great leaf, not far away. He landed on his hands and knees clumsily. His strong pinions drooped around him and trailed on the ground. For a moment he just knelt there, breathing heavily. His hawk eyes flashed yellow in the torchlight.

After a few seconds more, his arms and legs buckled beneath

him. They all watched him sink helplessly face down into the grass and lie still.

Everyone stayed frozen in place a bit longer. Then one of the bunjis whispered, "Good shot, Prago!" and the tension was released. They all started moving at once.

Hennelyn found herself irresistibly drawn to Arcmas's still form, with Nik following her. She knelt down near his head then cautiously reached a hand out to touch his shoulder. There was no reaction. He was fully and deeply under the sleeping properties of the drug, breathing evenly. Feeling bolder, Hennelyn grasped the helmet and pulled it off. His head lolled and came to rest with his right cheek upwards, eyes closed. She stroked the soft smooth feathers of his head and neck, accidentally smearing one fingertip in the small line of blood by his eyebrow. Her eyes filled with tears at the touch. Nik put a comforting hand on her back.

"Hennelyn, are you okay?" he asked gently.

"You were right, Nik..." she murmured, "he's no longer like the Arcmas that was my brother."

"Perhaps he's still in there somewhere and it will just take time. If he joins us like you were hoping..."

"I don't think he will. But we will see."

"Of course. And if anyone can convince him, it's you, Henna."

Nik moved away to quiet the horses, who had been rattled by all the fuss and flying about. Laria was being greeted by the other bunjis in quiet exultation. They were all touching their foreheads to greet her - a sign of respect, Hennelyn presumed. As though the Adon Miru had felt her gaze, she turned her head, looking straight across the little distance into Hennelyn's eyes, and smiled. Hennelyn smiled hesitantly back.

Grogo approached her and said, "The Aesthe will not sleep long. We were careful with the dose."

"All right, Grogo. Then we had better tie him up if I want to talk to him." Grogo eyed Arcmas's prone form uneasily.

"Will the rope we have be enough to hold him?"

"I brought wire for his hands."

"All right, Henlin. But we must not stay here too long. There may soon be pursuit," Grogo cautioned.

"It won't take long," Hennelyn assured him, eyeing him appealingly. "Arcmas wasn't always like this - like what you've just seen. I just want to give him a chance."

Grogo nodded his understanding.

"I know, Henlin. I'll get the others to help," he told her comfortingly. As he walked away, young Laria drew near.

"I really am glad to meet you, Henlin," she said in her soft voice. "Thank you for helping me. And the name of the other Sunchild?"

"Other...? Oh yes, that's Nik."

"...and Nik. I want to meet him too."

Laria's light blue eyes searched Hennelyn's, then she glanced at Arcmas and added, "Don't worry about him. Everything will happen as it is meant to. I will go to meet Nik."

She put a small hand on Hennelyn's shoulder before walking away.

Hennelyn didn't know how, but the warmth of Laria's touch seemed to sink into her body. Her worry inexplicably lessened and she felt calmer.

Hennelyn watched her go before she joined the bunjis in securely tying the unconscious Arcmas. They put him with his back against a poplar tree, his wrists brought behind him around its trunk and cinched securely together with the thick baling wire that Starkhon farmers used.

After that, most of the bunjis disappeared into the night, leaving only Grogo, Tuppin, Fraeling, and Brinkle as before, and Laria, Nik, and Hennelyn, of course. Fleeing with Laria would be easier in their own small group, and the other bunjis had a job to do, Grogo had told her. This was to confuse and mislead the enemy by laying a maze of trails to follow while he himself led the Adon Miru with Nik and Hennenlyn to safety.

# Chapter Twenty

When the night had just begun to take on a faint grey tinge with the coming dawn, Arcmas stirred and moaned softly. Awareness of the world around him seeped back slowly. He realized that he was sitting against a tree with his head hanging down. He lifted it with some difficulty and leaned it against the trunk. His forehead stung, and he felt a stiffened stickiness there just above his right eye. He was aware of a throbbing pain in his shoulders, and his head felt light and dizzy.

Slowly, he opened his golden hawk's eyes. The first thing he saw was the dim cottony shapes of unlit clouds above. Then, lowering his gaze, he saw small moving figures dotted about nearby. The realization flooded him that he was still among bunjis. There were only a few in the area now, either eating or gathering things up from the ground. His memory of what had happened and a feeling of urgency slammed back at the same time, and he tried to stand up swiftly. He couldn't. It was then that he understood why his arms seemed so awkward. It was a scary thought, but obviously a fact. He was tied up.

He struggled against the rope and wire in dismay, but it was no use. They held fast. He gave up suddenly with a grunt of frustration, breathing heavily. It was then that he noticed Hennelyn sitting on the ground over to his right, arms looped around her bent knees. Her summery blue eyes seemed to sparkle in the torchlight as she watched him. He slowly took in her familiar face and form. Somehow she looked more feminine now – less coltish and angular. Could she have changed so much in just a few months? Arcmas's eyes slid away from her steady gaze. He felt a twinge of conscience about his last words to her. But how could his own sister be a traitor? Maybe it was not true. Maybe this was all an elaborate plan to help the Starkhons rout out the bunjis...

His confusion and a ghost of his former anger made him slide his gaze away from hers and speak harshly. "Well, Hennelyn? What now? You've got what you wanted, it looks like. *And* me. What are you going to do next?"

"I want you to come with us, Arcmas," she answered shortly. Now he stared at her in astonishment.

"What? You're crazy! All of this is crazy. You won't get away

160

with this; you know that, don't you? In a very short time, they'll find the Adon Miru gone, and they'll come after you - if they haven't already started out. I knocked out the guard that was with her, but he's probably already awake by now."

"They don't even know what direction we've taken."

"They'll figure it out. You're missing. The Adon Miru's missing. And they'll see that I'm missing, too, pretty quick."

Hennelyn didn't answer. Then his voice softened until he sounded like the Arcmas she remembered.

"Let me go, Hennelyn. And come back with me along with the Adon Miru. We can put this night behind us," he said persuasively.

"I'm not going back, Arcmas. I know what Siras will want to do with me as well as you do. Especially if those 'rumors' you heard have named me as a traitor. Why do you want to go back anyway? They're only going to punish you for falling for my trick. Aren't they?"

She saw by a spasm of the muscles in his jaw that he knew she was right.

"It's my duty," was his stout answer. "We are Starkhons, Henna. And you - you're the general's daughter! You ought to know better - both back then and now. You should be remembering that your duty is to your father and your people. How can you be doing this?"

"What about you, Arcmas? Why didn't you come back to us, your family? If you had returned to us – to me – when you first got home, I would have told you everything. I wouldn't have tried to trick you."

"I am glad you didn't tell me your plan. I would have had to... I had my orders." He glared at her. "Don't you get it? I obeyed orders for all of us – for you and Father especially. At least I didn't turn traitor!" he spat. This time it was she who dropped her eyes.

"It's a long story, Arcmas. Five months ago..."

She had been going to say that the Arcmas of five months ago might have understood, but now she wasn't sure. She certainly saw, though, that she wasn't going to win him in a battle of words. She hopped up and turned sideways to him.

"You are right, I have betrayed," she said quietly into the air. "But at least I haven't killed."

Arcmas didn't answer and only watched as she moved away a few steps, grappling with many tormenting thoughts.

*What should I do now? How can I persuade him? There's no compromise that will work for us both; it's either my way or his. For Arcmas to join me would*

161

*be a great victory, but Arcmas against me… he could be my greatest enemy.*

As she was pondering, a sudden loud cry from behind made her wince. It was like the lonely scream of a hawk, but much greater in volume. She whirled around, catching him in the act as Arcmas let go with another similar call. Hennelyn swept the brightening sky with her eyes. When she saw what she was expecting, she ran for her bow and arrows.

The bunjis stared at both her and Arcmas with round eyes, startled. Hennelyn panted her way back to Arcmas's side. Something swished down between them with a rush of wings, and settled on Arcmas's one raised knee. It was a bald eagle, black with its white head glowing in the early morning light. It was huge. It leaned its curved beak close to Arcmas's face almost affectionately. Arcmas smiled at the bird.

"Isn't she magnificent?" he boasted. "This is my latest. I call her Whitefeather. Centenor Jakhron and I trained her together. When he sees her arrive at the Outpost, Jakhron will know I'm in trouble."

He lowered his cheek close to the bird's head, communing with her in the way that he had. Then, without warning, she flapped her way up into the air again, rising in slow circles. Without hesitation, Hennelyn readied her arrow and lifted it to point directly at the bird, easy to track in the moonlight brightened by the pearly grey of dawn.

"No, Hennelyn!" Arcmas cried out. She paid no attention. She was a better archer now than she was that day long ago when Arcmas had teased her about missing the target. She loosed the arrow with deadly accuracy. It struck Whitefeather squarely in the middle of her breast. She fell from the sky with a cry, landing almost at Laria's feet. The Adon Miru had walked out from the crowd and now stood close enough to hear Arcmas's and Hennelyn's next words.

Arcmas turned his head away from where Whitefeather lay sprawled on the ground.

"What's next, Hennelyn?" he burst out. His voice broke as he spoke. "Are you going to kill me, too?"

Again he struggled mightily but vainly against his tough wiry bonds. She stood with her bow lowered and her eyes down. She'd done what she had to do, but the remorse of bringing down such a spectacular bird, one that meant so much to her brother, was terrible. Her voice shook as she answered him.

"I'm sorry, Arcmas, I really am. I didn't want to. But I can't let you give us or the Adon Miru away. This means a great deal to my friends here. It's life and death to them. You know that."

## The Prisoner and the Traitor

Nik came up behind her and placed his hands on her sagging shoulders. He gazed at Arcmas with a mix of hostility and empathy.

Arcmas caught sight of him. "Oh, of course you've brought Nik into all of this, too. I should have guessed. And what about his family? You've marked them for punishment as well."

"I decided on my own," Nik replied coldly. "They know nothing. In fact, you can tell everyone that they know absolutely nothing!"

His angry tone surprised Hennelyn, until she realized he'd been very scared by the mention of his family.

Suddenly, to everyone's surprise, Laria approached. She passed Hennelyn and stopped just outside the reaching distance of Arcmas's taloned feet. He raised his head, and his amber eyes traveled up her clothing to rest on her face. Unexpectedly, he smiled wanly at her.

"You really are a brave girl," he said with genuine admiration, speaking the trade language. She smiled back. Then she glanced at Hennelyn and Nik behind her, and nodded at them significantly.

Hennelyn and Nik watched intently, ready to leap to the Adon Miru's protection if needed. Laria regarded Arcmas for a long moment, making the children wonder what she would do. They were astonished when Laria stepped around Arcmas's legs and knelt beside him. He looked at her curiously. She dampened a small rag with her canteen water, and gently wiped the dried blood from his forehead with it, revealing the small round wound the dart had made. As Arcmas blinked, she laid two of her fingers on the swollen bump and closed her eyes for a moment. Many of the bunjis were also watching now.

It seemed to Hennelyn that she saw a wavering blue glow around the small outstretched hand. It could have been a trick of the growing daylight. But when Laria lifted her fingertips, the wound was gone.

"You never did hurt me. I don't want you to have a scar there," she softly explained to Arcmas.

"But what did you- how did you - ?"

Laria didn't answer his question but spoke about another concern. "I am sorry that I must choose freedom rather than remain a prisoner of your tower. It's important to my own people that I stay with them. I wish you would change your mind and do as your friend asks. Or – isn't she your sister?"

"She was once," Arcmas muttered, with a dark glance in Hennelyn's direction. Laria shook her dark head sadly.

163

"She hasn't changed. It is you who have changed. There isn't a really important reason for you to refuse what she asks. I think that what we bunjis could offer you is far better than what you have known so far."

Arcmas sniffed at these words.

"Oh, really?"

Laria nodded. "Yes! Don't you want to be part of your own people again?" she asked.

"If all of you will let me loose, that's just where I'll be going!"

"I don't mean those people, those Fierce Ones. I mean your *real* people. The winged ones!"

The effect that these words had on Arcmas was frightening. His face drained of all color, and alarm flickered in his pale eyes, soon giving way to anger. His whole body grew rigid.

"You're lying," he accused her hoarsely, straining against his bonds. "Leave me alone!"

Laria stood up immediately. She said clearly, sounding hurt, "Adon Mirus don't lie. When you come to see the truth, I will be right there with you."

She walked away quickly, leaving Arcmas smarting with what appeared to him as an unforgivable cruelty, so quickly following her act of kindness.

The Starkhon youngsters moved away to find their packs, not knowing what to make of Laria's promise to Arcmas. They had no time to ponder it now, for it was high time to leave. The bunjis were already packed and waiting since they travelled very light.

Nik and Hennelyn turned the horses loose to let them find their way back home. Completing the preparations, they walked back to Arcmas.

"Well?" Hennelyn asked hopefully. "Have you decided to come with us yet?" She still spoke the trade language, so that all there could understand.

Arcmas slowly lifted his head and fixed them with a hostile glare she'd never seen on his face before.

"You're both traitors!" he spat out. "Liars and cheats. I'm not going anywhere with you."

Hennelyn's eyes misted a little, but Arcmas hadn't finished.

"I'm warning you, Hennelyn. If you let me go I'll come after you. They'll send me! You can't stop me unless you... kill me," he finished, breathing hard.

# The Prisoner and the Traitor

With a shock, Hennelyn saw that he was glancing quickly around at all of them, as though he really expected a sudden stroke of death.

"No one is going to hurt you, Arcmas," she told him sadly. "We'll let you go. But we need to drug you one more time. We just want you to sleep for a while so we can get on our way. I... I wish this could have ended better...."

She looked expectantly at Fraeling, who brought out a vial and sharp pointed dart from under his brown tunic. Arcmas glanced at it nervously. Fraeling moved quickly around behind Arcmas to reach his unfeathered hands. Just then, Arcmas flicked a wingtip out skillfully, attempting to knock the bunji down, but both wings were too hampered by the rope to do much. Fraeling dodged the maneuver with ease.

Arcmas grimaced when he felt the jab just above his thumb. The sleeping drug, developed especially by the bunjis to deal mercifully and quickly with large threatening predators, coursed through his veins and worked its usual rapid magic.

"Goodbye, Arcmas," Nik said from behind Hennelyn. Arcmas's only reaction was to glower.

Grimly he repeated, "I'll find you! I will!"

They watched his tense muscles slowly relax. His ragged breathing became gentle and even. Then his wary eyes closed, and his head began to nod. Very soon he was oblivious to the world once more, his head dropping back against the tree.

They waited a bit to make sure that he was really out – not just pretending – then unwound the bonds and wire from him. Nik and two of the bunjis caught him as he slumped sideways, and they laid him out comfortably on the ground.

"Will he be safe here?" Hennelyn worried. "Suppose a mountain lion or a bear –"

"Someone is watching," Grogo reassured her. "Don't you worry, Mistress, we are not all leaving. Arcmas will neither see nor smell the watchers when he awakens, but they will be near him until then."

She nodded, relieved. It was time to disappear – hopefully successfully. They all moved off together in a straggly line. At the rear, Nik glanced tentatively back at the feathery hump silhouetted in the deep early–morning shadow of the trees. It didn't stir, not even a little. He rubbed his tired eyes and followed along in the wake of the others.

Fraeling dropped back and took up the rear position behind Nik. The buckskin and white fur on the bunji figures melted into the landscape as they crept single file through the undergrowth.

The air was cold; it was one of those March days that relapsed back into winter instead of proceeding on with spring. Thick clouds blocked out the glory of the rising sun, and the sky was duller than the thin layer of bright, fresh snow laid down earlier. It was the time of year when Hennelyn always felt starved for the sight of something green.

The bunjis talked softly to each other and to the two young people as they walked along. They were traveling mostly within the woods in the little valley. It was a beautiful place. More than one spring bubbled out of the ground somewhere higher up, and these wound around in different trickles until they came together and made a little rivulet. This in turn made its way to swell the creek at the bottom of the valley. There were charming little waterfalls everywhere, still half encrusted with ice. But not even the snow-scorning crocuses poked their slumbering purple heads out of the frosty ground yet.

They crossed this wooded patch with its running water and climbed up out of the valley onto the prairie top. Before them lay the grasslands iced with new snow. Hennelyn hoped it would melt later to obscure their tracks. She felt less than confident still so near the Outpost. They all tried to step into one set of tracks to lessen the signs of their passing. Then Hennelyn remembered that other bunjis were supposedly laying all sorts of false trails elsewhere. She hoped it would be enough confusion to throw off the excellent Starkhon trackers. *The bunjis have done it before, haven't they?* she thought. *And it fooled us back then, too.*

As they walked along they saw a coyote or two and a number of deer, but no one pursued, yet. Around noon, they came to a large bog in the middle of their path and halted for the first time in a stand of thick bush for only a few minutes to have a small standing breakfast. All of them were weary from the sleepless night, but they went on anyway. Every mile they put behind them was an asset now.

Hennelyn could hardly believe that she had left home for good this time. She thought the last parting from the Outpost and Father had been hard, but this one threatened to tear a hole right through her, not visible from the outside but as painfully sharp as an arrow in her chest. After a moment, her steps faltered and then stopped entirely as she turned to look behind. Following, Nik and Fraeling stopped as well.

As Nik raised a drooping head, she saw her pain mirrored in his eyes. He was suffering as well, and saw that she shared it. He said nothing but looked back along the trail as well, as though to measure the distance he was getting from his family, with each step he took.

Fraeling understood, slowing as he approached them. Putting an arm around each teen's shoulder, he hugged them close in silent sympathy and then gently turned them around to face their future. His sad smile told them that though they were the only two humans in this group, they would not lack friends where they were going.

*Many new friends waiting to meet us,* Hennelyn thought hopefully. *And with these few friends here, now, who are beginning to feel like family.*

Linking arms with Nik, she helped him take the first few steps along this direction, this new way. This new life. She felt his body stiffen with resolve as he followed along, stepping a little faster, and they smiled at each other in spite of the unshed tears in their eyes.

To
Kristen Hubschmid and Kimberly Richardson

Your input was invaluable! Thank you.

## Note from the Author:

Hi!
You've just read an independently published book. I hope you liked
it!
If you want to know what happens to your favorite characters next,
read the second book in the series: Tower of the Deep Volume 2: The
Winged Warrior!

I would also love to know what you thought of Volume 1: The
Prisoner and the Traitor.
Please write a review in Kindle

If you are a Facebook user, you can check out and message me on
my FB author page:
A Voice Crying Publishers @h.m.richardson61

# About the Author

Born and raised in Edmonton, Alberta, Heidi Richardson later married a farmer and left the city life. Now tucked away on a farm northwest of Calgary, Heidi loves to tell stories, but she often says, "If there is a bright center to the publishing universe, I'm on the planet it's furthest from!" (Apologies to George Lucas and Star Wars fans!)

Through the decades, technology changed from laborious pen and paper to today's swift computers. Now she writes fictional fantasies for young readers, where her creative dreams weave with biblical truths to create allegorical visions.

Heidi's invitation to all her readers is, "Come dream with me."

Manufactured by Amazon.ca
Bolton, ON

27931578R00096